## *It was all going so well until that kiss.*

But when he'd got his arms around Katie and her mouth under his...he'd lost it. Every shred of control.

The bald truth was that Justin had seriously underestimated the power of his own feelings for the shy librarian with the adopted family he despised. It was funny, really—though he wasn't laughing. A royal backfire of his basic intention: *he* was supposed to seduce *her*.

Not the other way around.

What the hell was his problem here, anyway? He was getting way too invested in her. She had nothing to do with the main plan, and if she never let him get near her again it wouldn't matter in the least. So why should he care if she smiled at him again or not?

He decided he'd be better off not thinking too deeply on that one.

# Stranded with the Groom

## CHRISTINE RIMMER

SILHOUETTE®

SPECIAL EDITION™

First published in Great Britain 2006
Silhouette Books, Eton House, 18-24 Paradise Road,
Richmond, Surrey TW9 1SR

© Harlequin Books S.A. 2005

Special thanks and acknowledgement are given to Christine Rimmer
for her contribution to the MONTANA series.

ISBN 0 373 24657 9

23-0506

Printed and bound in Spain
by Litografia Rosés S.A., Barcelona

## CHRISTINE RIMMER

came to her profession the long way around. Before settling down to write about the magic of romance, she'd been everything from an actress to a phone sales representative to a playwright. Christine is grateful not only for the joy she finds in writing, but for what waits when the day's work is through: a man she loves, who loves her right back, and the privilege of watching their children grow and change day to day. She lives with her family in Oklahoma. Visit Christine at her new home on the web at www. christinerimmer.com.

For Montana readers everywhere.
Welcome to Thunder Canyon, Montana.

# Chapter One

"A mail-order bride," Katie Fenton muttered under her breath. "What were they *thinking*?"

In Thunder Canyon, Montana, it was the first Saturday after New Year's—and that meant it was Heritage Day.

The annual celebration, held in the big reception room of Thunder Canyon's sturdy stone-and-brick town hall, included rows of brightly decorated booths, some serving food and others displaying endless examples of local arts and crafts. There was always a pie auction and a quilt raffle and, as evening drew on, a potluck supper and dancing late into the night.

Also, this year, the Thunder Canyon Historical Society had decided to put on a series of historical reenactments. In the morning, they'd presented the local legend of the great Thunder Bird, a mythical figure who took the form of a man every spring and met his mortal mate on sacred ground. According to Native American lore, their joyous reunion caused the spring rains to fall, the leaves and flowers to emerge and the grass to grow lush and green.

At two in the afternoon, there was the discovery of gold in 1862 at Grasshopper Creek—complete with rocks the size of baseballs, sprayed gold to look like huge nuggets.

And now, at four-thirty, it was time for the mail-order bride—played by Katie—arriving by train to meet and marry a man she'd never seen before.

Katie stood huddled on the narrow stage at the west end of the hall. Perched on a makeshift step behind a rickety cardboard mock-up of a steam engine and a red caboose, she kept her shoulders hunched and her head down so she couldn't be seen over the top of the fake train.

Utterly miserable—Katie hated, above all, to make a spectacle of herself—she stared at the door hole cut in the caboose. On cue, she was supposed to push it open and emerge to meet her "groom."

Outside, the wind howled. A storm was blowing in. Though the local weatherman had promised nothing much worse than a few flurries, most of the Heritage Day crowd had departed the hall during the past half hour or so and headed for the safety of their homes.

Katie herself was more than ready to call it a day.

But unfortunately, this year for the Heritage Day revels, a local merchant had come up with the bright idea of providing free beer on tap. The beer booth was a big hit. Certain of the citizenry had been knocking it back since eleven or so. They couldn't have cared less that the predicted flurries seemed to be shaping up into a full-blown blizzard. They were too busy having a grand old time.

Out on the main floor, someone let out a whistle. Katie heard the impatient stomping of heavy feet on the old, well-polished hardwood floorboards.

"C'mon, where's the bride?"

"Get on with it. We want the bride!"

"The bride!"

"The bride! Give us the bride!"

Katie cast a desperate glance to the tiny wing area at the edge of the stage where sweet old Emelda Ross, one of the few members of the Historical Society who'd yet to go home, hovered over an ancient reel-to-reel tape recorder.

"The bride, the bride!"

"Wahoo, let's see her!"

Katie gave Emelda a shaky nod. Emelda turned on the tape and two loud train whistles erupted: her cue.

Sucking in a big breath and letting it out slowly, Katie tugged on her 1880s-style merino wool frock, adjusted her bonnet and pushed open the cardboard door.

The beer drinkers erupted into a chorus of catcalls and stomping.

"The librarian!" one of them shouted. "Hey, the librarian is the mail-order bride!"

Another let out a whoop. "Hey, Katie! Welcome to Thunder Canyon!"

"We love you, Katie!"

"If your groom stands you up, I'll take you, Katie!"

Lovely.

With care, so as not to knock over the train, Katie emerged to face the crowd. She smoothed her dress again, her nervous hands shaking. How, she wondered miserably, had she let herself get roped into this one?

With great effort, she forced a wobbly smile and waved at the beer drinkers, who obligingly clapped and stomped all the louder. She stared out over the seventy or so grinning faces—many of them looking downright woozy by then—and longed to be anywhere but there.

It was all dear old Ben Saunders's fault. The high school history teacher had been the one to propose the mail-order bride reenactment. The Historical Society went wild for the idea—all except for Katie, who was lukewarm on the concept at best.

Since most of Katie's fellow society members were well into their forties at least and the other two younger ones were already slated to play the legendary Thunder Bird and his mortal love, it was decided that Katie should play the bride.

She had tried to say no, but who listened? *No one,* that's who. And now, here she was, alone in front of the cardboard train, a ludicrous spectacle for the Heritage Day beer drinkers to whistle and holler at.

Ben himself was supposed to be her groom. Unfortunately, the history teacher had awakened that morning with terrible stomach cramps. He'd been rushed to Thunder Canyon General for an emergency appendectomy. And then, when the sky darkened and the wind came up and the first snowflakes began to fall, pretty much everyone from the society except Emelda had decided to go home. *They* made the plans and now Katie stood on the stage alone, shaking with nerves and stuck with the follow-through.

Since her ''groom'' was in the hospital, she'd almost succeeded in canceling this ridiculous display. But then, a half hour ago, an out-of-towner named Justin Caldwell had agreed to step in and take Ben's part. Caldwell was a business associate of Caleb Douglas—Caleb being a local mover and shaker who owned half the property for miles around and also happened to be a second father to Katie. Caleb had ribbed the stranger into playing the groom. The poor guy resisted at first, but when Caleb kept after him, he couldn't refuse.

And speaking of Justin Caldwell...

Where was he?

Frantically, Katie scanned the noisy crowd for her impromptu pretend groom. Good gravy. In a moment, one of the drunken men down on the floor would be staggering up to take his place.

But no—there he was.

He stood off to the left, at the edge of the crowd, wearing the ill-fitting old-time garb—complete with silly red suspenders and clunky nineteenth-century-style boots—intended for the potbellied Ben Saunders. Katie met the stranger's piercing blue eyes and a crazy little thrill shivered through her. Even in the ridiculous outfit, the guy still somehow managed to look absolutely gorgeous. She felt the grateful smile as it quivered across her mouth. If she had to make a fool of herself, at least it would be with the best-looking man in the hall. And beyond being handsome, there was the added attraction that he appeared to be sober.

''The groom!'' someone shouted. ''Where's the damn groom?''

''Right here,'' Justin Caldwell answered easily in a deep, firm voice. He took off his floppy felt hat and waved it high for all of them to see.

''Get up there and claim your bride!''

''Yeah, man. Don't keep her waiting!''

Justin Caldwell obliged. He mounted the steps at the side of the stage and came toward Katie, his long strides purposeful and confident. When he reached her, he gallantly swept off the floppy hat a second time. Her overtaxed heart raced faster still.

And then, of all things, he reached for her hand. Before she could jerk it away, he brought it to his full-lipped mouth.

Katie stood stunned, staring into those gleaming blue eyes of his, every nerve in her body cracking and popping, as he placed a tender kiss on the back of her hand.

The crowd went wild.

''That's the way you do it!''

''Oh, yeah!''

''Way to go!''

His lips were so warm—and his hand firm and dry. Her hand, she knew, was clammy and shaking. Gulping, Katie carefully pulled her fingers free.

Caleb's business partner nodded and put his absurd hat back on. He looked so calm. As if he did this sort of thing every day. He leaned in closer, bringing with him the subtle scent of expensive aftershave. "Now, what?" he whispered in that velvety voice of his.

"Uh, well, I…" Katie gulped again. She just knew her face was flaming red.

"Kiss 'er!" someone shouted. "Lay a big, smackin' one right on 'er!"

Everyone applauded the idea, causing Katie to silently vow that next year, under no circumstances, would there be free beer.

"Yeah," someone else hollered. "A kiss!"

"A big, wet, juicy one! Grab 'er and give it to 'er!"

Justin Caldwell, bless him, did no such thing. He did lift a straight raven-black eyebrow. "The natives are becoming restless," he said low. "We'd better do *something.…*"

*Do something.* His soft words echoed in her frazzled mind. "The, uh, ceremony…"

He smiled then, as if mildly amused. "Of course." He suggested, "And for that we would need…" He let his voice trail off, giving her an opportunity to fill in the blank.

She did. "The preacher." Her throat locked up. She coughed to clear it. "Uh. Right."

"Get on with it!" someone yelled.

"Yeah! Get a move on. Let's see the rest of the show!"

Outside, a particularly hard gust of wind struck the high-up windows and made them rattle. Nobody seemed to notice. They kept laughing and clapping.

"So where is this preacher?" her "groom" inquired.

"Um, well…" Katie wildly scanned the crowd again. Where was Andy Rickenbautum? The balding, gray-haired retired accountant was supposed to step up and declare himself a circuit preacher and "marry" them, but Katie couldn't see him among the crowd. Evidently, like most of the Historical Society members, he'd headed home.

Maybe Caleb, who'd gotten such a kick out of the whole thing, could help out and play Andy's part.…

But no. Caleb appeared to be gone, too. And Adele, his wife, who had taken in a teenaged Katie and raised her as her own, was nowhere to be seen, either. Now what?

At the Heritage Museum several blocks away, the society had set up a wedding "reception," complete with finger food and beverages and an opportunity for folks to see up-close the artifacts of the life the mail-order bride and her groom would have lived. The idea was to lure everyone over there behind the "bride" and "groom," in the museum's prized refurbished buckboard carriage. They'd all enjoy the snacks, look around—hopefully make a donation—and then head on back to the hall for the potluck supper and dancing that would follow.

But without the fake wedding first, how could they hold a pretend reception?

A couple of the beer drinkers had figured that out. One of them yelled, "Hey! Where's the preacher?"

"Yeah! We need the dang preacher to get this thing moving!"

What a disaster, Katie thought. It was definitely time to give up and call the whole thing off.

Katie forced herself to face the crowd. "Ahem. Excuse me. I'm afraid there's no one to play the preacher and we're just going to have to—"

A resonant voice from the back of the crowd cut her off. "Allow me to do the honors." Every head in the room swiveled toward the sound. The source, an austere-looking bearded fellow, announced, "I'd be proud to unite such a handsome couple in the sacred bonds of matrimony."

Someone snickered. "And just who the hell are you?"

The tall fellow, all dressed in black, made his way to the front of the crowd. He mounted the steps and came to stand with Katie and her "groom." "The Reverend Josiah Green, at your service, miss," he intoned. He dipped his head at Katie, then turned to Justin. "Sir."

Someone broke into a laugh. "Oh, yeah. *Reverend.* That's a good one...."

"He's perfect," someone else declared. "He even looks like a real preacher."

Looking appropriately grave, the "reverend" bowed to the crowd. The usual whistles and catcalls followed. "Reverend" Green turned his gaze to the spindle-legged antique table a few feet from the cardboard train. "I see you have everything ready." On the table, courtesy of the Historical Society, waited a Bible, a valuable circa-1880 dip pen and matching inkwell and a copy of an authentic late-nineteenth-century marriage license.

Emelda, smiling sweetly, emerged from the wings. A smattering of applause greeted her as she got the Bible and handed it to the "reverend."

"Ahem," said the "reverend." "If you'll stand here. And you here..." Katie, Justin and Emelda moved into the positions Mr. Green indicated.

The man in black opened the old Bible. A hush fell over the crowd as he instructed, "Will the bride and groom join hands?" Caldwell removed his hat. He dropped it to the stage floor, took Katie's hand and gave her an encouraging smile. She made herself smile back and didn't jerk away, in spite of the way his touch caused a tingling all through her, a sensation both embarrassing and scarily exciting.

The fake preacher began, "We are gathered here together..."

It was so strange, standing there on the narrow wooden stage with the cardboard train behind them and the wind howling beyond the stone walls as the pretend reverend recited the well-known words of the marriage ceremony.

The rowdy crowd stayed quiet. And the words themselves were so beautiful. Green asked if there was anyone present who saw any reason that Justin and Katie should not be joined. No one made a sound. If not for the wind, you could have heard a feather whispering its way to the floor. Green said, "Then we shall proceed...."

And Katie and the stranger beside her exchanged their pretend vows. When the "reverend" said, "I now pronounce you husband and wife," Katie had to gulp back tears.

Really, this whole weird situation was making her way too emotional.

"You may kiss the bride."

Oh, God. The kiss…

It hadn't seemed so bad when it was only good old Ben. But Justin Caldwell was another story. He was just so good-looking, so exactly like the kind of man any woman would want to kiss.

Truth was, Katie wouldn't mind kissing him. Not at all. Under different circumstances.

Maybe. If they ever came to really know each other…

Oh, why was she obsessing over this? The final vow-sealing kiss was part of the program. It wouldn't be much of a pretend wedding without it.

*Almost over,* Katie silently promised herself as Caldwell turned to face her. With a small, tight sigh, she lifted her chin. Pressing her eyes shut and pursing up her mouth, she waited for her "groom" to lean down and give her a quick, polite peck.

The peck didn't happen. Warily, she opened her right eye to a slit. Caldwell was looking down at her, apparently waiting for her to look at him. When he saw she was peeking, one corner of that full mouth of his quirked up and he winked at her.

A ridiculous giggle forced its way up in her throat and almost got away from her. She gulped it back, straightened her head and opened both eyes. At the same time as she was controlling her silly urge to laugh, the man before her reached out his hand. He did it so slowly and carefully, she didn't even flinch.

He took the end of the bow that tied her bonnet under her chin. One little tug and the bow fell away.

Gently, he guided the bonnet from her head. Her brown curls, which she'd hastily shoved in beneath the hat, fell loose to her shoulders. Justin—all of a sudden, she found she was mentally calling him by his first name—tossed the hat to Emelda and then, with tender, careful fingers, he smoothed her hair.

Oh, God. Her throat had gone tight. She felt as if she would cry again. This pretending to get married was darned hard on her nerves—or maybe she had a little natural-born performer in her, after all. Maybe she was simply "getting into" her part.

Their formerly boisterous audience remained pin-drop quiet. How did people in the theater put it? The phrase came to her. She and Justin had the crowd *in the palms of their hands....*

Justin braced a finger under her chin and she took his cue, lifting her mouth for him.

His dark head descended and his lips—so gently—covered hers.

That did it. The Heritage Day revelers burst into wild applause, sharp whistles, heavy stomping and raucous catcalls.

Katie hardly even heard them. She was too wrapped up in Justin's kiss. It was a kiss that started out questioning and moved on to tender and from there to downright passionate.

Oh, my goodness! Did he know how to kiss or what? She grabbed onto his broad, hard shoulders and kissed him back for all she was worth.

When he finally pulled away, she stared up at him,

dazed. He had those blue, blue eyes. Mesmerizing eyes. She could drown in those eyes and never regret being lost....

"Ahem," said the "reverend," good and loud, gazing out over the audience with a look of stern disapproval until they quieted again. "There remains the documentation to attend to."

Katie blinked and collected herself, bringing a hand up and smoothing her hair. Justin turned to face Josiah Green, who had crossed to the spindle-legged table. He picked up the old pen and dipped it in the ink and expertly began filling out the fake marriage license. "That's Katie...?"

"Fenton."

"Speak up, young lady."

"Katherine Adele Fenton." She said her whole name that time, nice and clear, and then she spelled it for him.

"And Justin...?"

"Caldwell." He spelled his name, too.

They acted it all out as if it were the real thing, filling in all the blanks, signing their names. When the "reverend" called for another witness besides Emelda, one of the guys from down on the floor jumped right up onto the stage and signed where Josiah Green pointed.

When the last blank line had been filled in, Green expertly applied the sterling silver rocker blotter. Then he held up the license for all to see. "And so it is that yet another young and hopeful couple are happily joined in holy wedlock."

As the clapping and stomping started up again,

Emelda stepped forward. She waited, looking prim and yet indulgent, her wrinkled hands folded in front of her, until the noise died down. Then she announced that, weather permitting, there was to be a reception at the Heritage Museum over on Elk Avenue. "Everyone is welcome to attend. Help yourself to the goodies—and don't forget that donation box. We count on all of you to make the museum a success. Just follow the bride and groom in their authentic buckboard carriage."

Evidently, the crowd found that suggestion too exciting to take standing still. They surged up onto the stage and surrounded the small wedding party, jostling and jumping around, knocking over the cardboard train and almost upsetting the antique table with its precious load of vintage writing supplies. Laughing and shouting, they tugged and coaxed and herded Katie and Justin down the stage steps, across the main floor and out into the foyer.

Katie laughed and let herself be dragged along. By then, the crazy situation had somehow captured her. The day's events had begun to seem like some weird and yet magical dream. Her lips still tingled from the feel of Justin's mouth on hers. And she was pleased, she truly was, that her little reenactment, skirting so close to disaster, had ended up a great success.

In the foyer, the crowd surged straight for the double doors that opened directly onto the covered wooden sidewalk of Old Town's Main Street. They pushed the doors wide and a blinding gust of freezing wind and snow blew in, making everyone laugh all the louder.

"Brrrr. It's a cold one."

"Yep. She's really movin' in."

"Gonna be one wild night, and that's for certain."

The snow swirled so thick, the other side of Main Street was nothing more than a vague shadow through the whiteness. The horse, a palomino mare, and the buckboard were there, waiting, the reins thrown and wrapped around one of the nineteenth-century-style hitching posts that ran at intervals along Main at the edge of the sidewalk, bringing to mind an earlier time.

Katie herself had requested the horse, whose name was Buttercup. The mare belonged to Caleb. He kept a fine stable of horses out at the family ranch, the Lazy D. A sweet-natured, gentle animal, Buttercup was getting along in years—and, boy, did she look cold. Icicles hung from her mouth. She glanced toward the crowd and snorted good and loud, as if to say, *Get me out of this. Now…*

Really, maybe they ought to slow down here. The snow did look pretty bad.

"Um, I think that we ought to…" She let the sentence die. She'd always had a too-soft voice. And no one was listening, anyway.

The revelers herded her and Justin into the old open, two-seater carriage. It creaked and shifted as it took their weight.

"Use the outerwear and the blankets under the seat!" Emelda shouted from back in the doorway to the hall foyer. A frown had deepened the creases in her brow. Maybe she was having her doubts about this, too.

But then Emelda put on a brave smile and waved

and the wind died for a moment. Really, it was only two blocks west and then three more northeast to the museum. And, according to the weather reports, the storm *was* supposed to blow itself out quickly.

It should be okay.

Justin brushed the snow from a heavy ankle-length woolen coat—a tightly fitted one with jet buttons down the front and a curly woolen ruff at the neck. He helped her into it, then put on the rough gray man's coat himself. There was a Cossack-style hat for her that matched the ruff at her neck. No hat for Justin, and he'd left the silly, floppy one back in the hall. But he didn't seem to mind. There were heavy gloves for both of them.

They shook out the pile of wool blankets and wrapped up in them. Justin pulled on his gloves and Josiah Green handed him the reins.

"Bless you, my children," Green intoned, as if the marriage vows he'd just led them through had been for real.

"Thanks," Justin muttered dryly. "Looks like we'll need it." He glanced at Katie. "Okay…" He had a you-got-us-into-this kind of look on his handsome face. "Where to?"

"If you want, I'll be glad to take the reins."

"I can handle it. Where to?"

Even if he didn't know what he was doing, it should be all right, she thought. Buttercup was patient and docile as they come. "Straight ahead. Then you'll turn right on Elk, about three blocks down."

"What? I can't hear you."

She forced herself to raise her voice and repeated the instructions.

Justin shook the reins and clicked his tongue and Buttercup started walking. Her bridle, strung with bells, tinkled merrily as they set off, the beer-sodden townsfolk cheering them on.

The wind rose again, howling, and the snow came down harder.

A half block later, the thick, swirling flakes obscured the hall and the knot of cheering rowdies behind them. A minute or two after that, Katie couldn't hear their voices. All at once, she and this stranger she'd just pretended to marry were alone in a whirling vortex of white.

Katie glanced over her shoulder. She saw nothing but swirling snow and the shadows of the buildings and cars on either side of Main.

The snow fell all the harder. It beat at them, borne by the hard-blowing wind. Katie huddled into the blankets, her cheekbones aching with the cold.

Buttercup plodded on, the snow so thick that when Katie squinted into it, she could barely see the horse's sleek golden rump. She turned to the man beside her. He seemed to sense her gaze on him. He gave her a quick, forced kind of smile—his nose was Rudolph-red, along with his cheeks and chin and ears—and then swiftly put his focus back on the wall of white in front of them.

For a split second, she spied a spot of red to the side—the fire hydrant at the corner of Elk and Main. Wasn't it? "Turn right! Here!" Katie shouted it out good and loud that time. Justin tugged the reins and the horse turned the corner.

They passed close to the fire hydrant. Good. This was the right way. And as long as they were on Elk Avenue now, they'd literally run into the museum—a sprawling red clapboard building that had started out its existence as the Thunder Canyon School. It sat on a curve in the street, where Elk Avenue made a sharp turn due east.

The palomino mare slogged on into the white. By then, Katie couldn't see a thing beyond the side rails of the buckboard and Buttercup's behind.

Good Lord. Were they lost? It was beginning to look that way.

Hungry for reassurance, Katie shouted over the howling wind, "We *are* still on Elk Avenue, aren't we?"

Justin shouted back, "I'm from out of town, remember? Hate to tell you, but I haven't got a clue."

## Chapter Two

Just as Katie began to fear they'd somehow veered off into the open field on the west side of Elk Avenue, the rambling red clapboard building with its wide front porch loomed up to the left.

"We're here!" she yelled, thrilled at the sight.

Justin tugged the reins and the horse turned into the parking lot. Ten or twelve feet from the front porch, the buckboard creaked to a stop—at which point it occurred to Katie that they couldn't leave poor Buttercup out in this. "Go around the side! There's a big shed out back."

He frowned at her.

She shouted, "The horse. We need to put her around back—to the left."

His frown deepened. She could see in those blue eyes that he thought Buttercup's comfort was the least of their problems right then. But he didn't argue. Shoulders hunched into his ugly old-fashioned coat, he flicked the reins and Buttercup started moving again.

When they got to the rear of the building, Katie signaled him on past a long, narrow breezeway and around to the far side of the tall, barnlike shed. "I'll open up," she yelled and pushed back the blankets to swing her legs over the side. She opened the gate that enclosed a small paddock northwest of the shed. Justin drove the buckboard through and she managed to shut the gate.

The snow was six or eight inches deep already. It dragged at her heavy skirts and instantly began soaking her delicate ankle-high lace-up shoes as she headed for the shed doors around back. How did women do it, way back when? She couldn't help but wonder. There were some situations—this one, for instance—when a woman really needed to be wearing a sturdy pair of trousers and waterproof boots.

There was a deep porchlike extension running the length of the shed at the rear, sheltering the doors. She ducked under the cover, stomping her shoes on the frozen ground and shaking the snow off her hem. Even with gloves on, her hands were so stiff with cold, it took forever to get the combination padlock to snap open. But eventually, about the time she started thinking her nose would freeze and fall off, the shackle popped from the case. She locked it onto the hasp.

And then, though the wind fought her every step of the way, she pulled back one door and then the other, latching them both to hooks on the outside wall, so they wouldn't blow shut again. She gestured Justin inside and he urged the old mare onward.

Katie followed the buckboard inside as Justin hooked the reins over the back of the seat and jumped to the hard-packed dirt floor. "Cold in here." He rubbed his arms and stomped his feet, looking around, puzzled, as Buttercup shook her head and the bells tinkled merrily. "What is this?"

"Kind of a combination garage and barn. The Historical Society is planning on setting it up as a model of a blacksmith's shop." She indicated the heavy, rusting iron equipment against the walls and on the plank floor. "For right now, it'll do to stable Buttercup 'til this mess blows over." There were several oblong bales of hay stacked under the window, waiting to be used for props in some of the museum displays. Buttercup whickered at them hopefully.

"Go on through there." Katie indicated the door straight across from the ones she'd left open. It led to the breezeway and the museum. "It's warm inside. And a couple of ladies from the Historical Society should be in there waiting, with the food and drinks."

He looked at her sideways. "What about you?"

She was already trudging over to unhook Buttercup from the buckboard. "I learned to ride on this horse, I'll have you know. I'm going to get her free of this rig and make her comfortable until someone from the ranch can come for her."

"The ranch?"

"She's Caleb's, from out at the Lazy D."

He stomped his feet some more, making a big show

of rubbing his arms. "Can't someone inside take care of the horse?"

"Anna Jacks and Tildy Matheson were supposed to set out the refreshments for the 'wedding reception.' They're both at least eighty."

"Maybe someone else has shown up by now."

Doubtful, she thought. And even if they had, they'd most likely be drunk. "I'd rather just do it myself before I go in."

He gave her an appraising kind of look and muttered, heavy on the irony, "And you seemed so shy, back there at the hall."

She stiffened. Yes, okay. As a rule, she *was* a reserved sort of person. But when something needed doing, Katie Fenton didn't shirk. She hitched up her chin and spoke in a carefully pleasant tone. "You can go on inside. I'll be there as soon as I'm through here."

He insisted on helping her. So she set him the task of searching for a box cutter in the drawers full of rusting tools on the west wall. When he found one, she had him cut the wire on a couple of the bales and spread the hay. Meanwhile, she unhitched Buttercup from the rig, cleaned off the icicles from around her muzzle and wiped her down with one of the blankets from the buckboard.

"Okay," she said when the job was done. "Let's go in."

He headed for the still-open doors to the pasture. "I'll just shut these."

"No. Leave them open. The walls cut most of the wind, so it won't be too cold in here. And Buttercup can move around a little, and have access to the snow when she gets thirsty.''

He shrugged and turned to follow her out—which was a problem as the door to the breezeway was locked from the outside. They ended up having to go out the big doors. Hunched into the wind, with the snow stinging their faces, they slogged through the deepening snow around the side of the shed and back through the gate that enclosed the paddock.

Once under the partial shelter of the breezeway, they raced for the back door, the wind biting at them, tearing at Katie's heavy skirts.

It was locked. Katie knocked good and hard. No one came.

Justin wore a bleak look. ''What now?''

''No problem.'' Katie took off her right glove and felt along the top of the door frame, producing the key from the niche there. She held it up for him to see before sticking it in the lock and pushing the door inward onto an enclosed back porch. He signaled her ahead of him and followed right after, pulling the door closed to seal out the wind and snow.

By then, it had to be after six. It was pretty dark. Katie flipped on the porch light and gestured at the hooks lining the wall next to the door that led inside. ''Hang up your coat,'' she suggested, as she set her gloves on a small table and began undoing the jet buttons down her front. The porch wasn't heated and she shivered as the coat fell open. ''Whew. Cold…''

''I hope it's warm in there.''

''It is,'' she promised as she shrugged out of the long gray coat and hung it on a hook. He hung his beside it. She swiped off her hat, shook out her hair and tossed the hat on a porch chair.

"This way." Katie unlocked the door and pushed it open into the museum's small, minimally equipped kitchen area. Lovely warm air flowed out and surrounded them.

"Much better," Justin said from behind her.

She led him in, hanging the key on the waiting hook by the door and turning on the light.

The long counter was spotless, and so was the table over by the side windows. A few cups dried on a mat at the sink. No sign of Tildy or Anna.

They moved on into the big central room, which a hundred years before had been the only schoolroom. The room was now the museum's main display area—and pitch-dark. Years ago, when rooms were added on around it, the windows had been closed up. Katie felt for the dimmer switch near the door, turning it up just enough that they could see where they were going.

The light revealed roped-off spaces containing nineteenth-century furniture arranged into living areas: a bedroom, a weaving room, a parlor, a one-room "house" with all the living areas combined, the furniture in that section rough-hewn, made by pioneer hands.

"No sign of your friends," Justin said.

"They probably got worried about the storm and went home."

A quick check of the two other display rooms confirmed their suspicions. They were alone.

"No cars out there," Justin said once they'd

reached the front reception area, where trays of sandwiches, cookies and coffee, tea and grape drink waited for the crowd that wasn't coming. "Remember? The parking lot in front of the building. It was empty." She did remember, now that he mentioned it. He asked, "What now?"

It was a good question; too bad she had no answer to it. "I guess we wait."

"For?"

She wished she knew. "For the storm to die down a little so we can leave?"

He gave her a humorless half smile. "Was that an answer—or just another question?"

Katie put up both hands, palms up. "Oh, really. I just don't know."

Justin studied her for a moment, wearing an expression she couldn't read. Then, out of nowhere, he plunked himself down into one of the reception chairs and started pulling off his boots.

The sight struck her as funny, for some crazy reason. She laughed—and then felt stupid for doing it when he glanced up from under the dark shelf of his brow, his full-lipped mouth a grim line. "These damn boots are at least a size too small."

Katie winced. "Sorry."

With a grunt, he tugged off a boot. "For what?"

She sank to a chair herself. "Oh, you know. Caleb shouldn't have roped you into this. And I should have spoken up and called the whole thing off."

He dropped the boot to the floor, pulled off the other one and set it down, too. "Are you capable of that?"

"Excuse me?"

That dry smile had gone devilish. "Speaking up."

She sat straighter and brushed a bit of lint off her skirt. "Now and then, absolutely."

His smile got wider. "Like with the horse."

She nodded. "That's right." Blowing out a weary breath, she let her shoulders slump again. "But back in the hall—oh, I just hate getting up in front of a lot of people. Especially a lot of people who've had too much beer."

"I hear you on that one." He looked down at his heavy wool socks—and wiggled his toes. "Now, that's more like it."

Her own feet were kind of pinched in the narrow lace-up shoes. What the heck? She hiked up her soggy skirts—which gave off the musty scent of wet wool— and set to work on the laces. When she had both shoes off, she set them neatly beside her chair, smoothed her skirt down and straightened to find him watching her. There was humor in his eyes and something else, something much too watchful. She found herself thinking, *What's he up to?* And then instantly chided herself for being suspicious.

What *could* he be up to? Except wishing he hadn't let Caleb talk him into this.

The watchful look had faded from his face as if it had never been. He asked softly, "Now, isn't that better?"

"What?"

"Without your shoes…"

She felt a smile tug at her mouth. Oh, really, he was much too good-looking for her peace of mind.

She answered briskly, "Yes, it is." And she picked up a tray of sandwich triangles from the reception desk. "Help yourself. It's probably the closest thing to dinner we're going to get."

He took one and bit into it. "Ham and American. With mayo. The best."

"Oh, I'll bet." She took one for herself and gestured at the big stainless steel coffee urn, the hot water for tea and the glass pitcher of grape drink. "And coffee. Or a cold drink…"

He got up. "You?"

"Coffee sounds good. With a little cream."

He poured them each a cup, splashed cream from a little stoneware pitcher into hers and handed it over with a courtly, "Mrs. Caldwell."

She played along. "*Mr.* Caldwell." Really, she was grateful he was taking this so calmly.

He sank into his chair again and sipped the hot brew. "Now we're married, I think you're going to have to call me Justin."

She had that silly, nervous urge to laugh again. She quelled it. "By all means. And please. Call me Katie. I firmly believe married people should be on a first-name basis with each other."

"I agree. Katie." He finished off the rest of his sandwich. She held out the tray and he took another. She took one, too. He asked, "So how was that train ride?"

She rolled her eyes. "I should have taken a club car."

About then, the false cheer they were both trying to keep up deserted them. They sat silent, like the strangers they really were, eating their sandwiches, listening to the wind whistling in the eaves outside.

Eventually, he turned to her, his expression grave. "Will anyone else show up?"

"In this?" She gestured at the six-over-six front windows. Beyond the golden glow of the porch light, there was only darkness and hard-blowing snow. "I don't think so."

He turned and looked at the round institutional-style clock on the wall above the desk. It was six thirty-five. "How long will we be stuck here?"

He *would* have to ask that. She cleared her throat. "Maybe, if we're lucky, the snow will stop soon."

"And if it doesn't?"

Katie sighed. "Good question. We'll just have to wait and see how bad it gets."

"Should we call someone, let them know we arrived here and we're safe?" He felt in his pockets. "Damn…"

"What?"

"I left my cell in my own clothes, back at the hall." He produced a handsome calfskin wallet and waved at her. "The good news is I've got plenty of cash."

Katie forced a grin. "Whew. I was worried. What if we wanted to do a little shopping?" He made a sound halfway between a grunt and a chuckle, and she added, on a more somber note, "And cell phones don't work all that well around these parts, anyway. Lots of mountains. Not many cell towers."

"I knew that," he said, his mouth twisting wryly.

She set her coffee cup on the edge of the reception

desk, reached for the phone and put it to her ear. "Dead." Carefully, she set it back in its cradle.

"Terrific."

"Count your blessings," she advised, trying to keep things positive. "At least we still have heat and electricity. And plenty of water, as long as the pipes don't freeze."

He didn't look too reassured, but he got the message. "Right. Might as well look on the bright side."

"Exactly."

Rising, he went to the trays of food and chose another sandwich.

The museum had propane heat throughout, but there was also the remains of a fire in the potbellied stove in the corner. Katie got up and put in another log. She jabbed it with the poker until it was well nestled in the bright coals. The red flames licked up.

She shut the stove door and turned—to find him watching her again. "Is something the matter?"

He frowned. "No. Of course not—well, except for the situation we're in here."

"You keep looking at me strangely."

His gaze remained far too watchful—for a moment. And then he shrugged. "Forgive me. I'm just... curious about you, I guess. Caleb Douglas told me you're the 'little girl he never had.' He raised you, I take it?"

She had no idea why she felt reluctant to answer him. What was there to hide? She said, "My mother and Adele were both from Philadelphia, best friends at Bryn Mawr—you did meet Addy, didn't you?"

"I did." He looked like he was waiting to hear more.

So she elaborated. "They had an instant connection, my mother and Addy, from the way Addy tells it. And their families were friends. When my parents died, I was fourteen. There was really no one left in my immediate family to take me. Addy came and got me." Katie smiled at the memory—Adele, with her suitcases at her feet in the foyer of the Center City brownstone near Rittenhouse Square that had belonged to Katie's grandparents and their parents before them. When Katie came down the stairs to meet her, Adele held out her arms, her blue eyes shining with tears....

Katie swallowed down the emotion the memory brought with it and Justin asked, "Adele brought you here, then—to Thunder Canyon?"

"That's right, to live with her and Caleb."

"And you loved it."

"Yes, I did. From the first."

"Because?"

She hesitated. Could he really want to hear all this? But he was looking at her expectantly. So she told him, "It was...just what I'd needed. A close-knit community, where people looked out for each other. I lived at the Lazy D through my teenage years, went to Thunder Canyon High and then on to college in Colorado. As Caleb told you, he and Addy never had a daughter, so it worked out beautifully. For all of us."

"All?"

"Caleb. Addy. And Riley. Have you met Riley?"

He nodded. "Their son. Caleb introduced me to him a few days ago—and I suppose he's like a big brother to you?"

She picked up her soggy skirt so it wouldn't drag on the floor and padded to one of the front windows, where she looked out at the porch, the darkness and the driving snow beyond. "Yes. I think of Riley like a brother...." She turned back to him. "They're fine people." Did she sound defensive? A little. She wasn't really sure why. Something hostile in the way he'd spoken of Riley, maybe.

But why in the world would Justin Caldwell be hostile toward Riley, whom he'd only just met? Clearly, the stress of their situation was getting to her, making her read things into his tone that weren't there.

She tried for a lighter note. "Caleb is so pleased that you've invested in his ski resort." Caleb had always been a wheeler-dealer. The resort was a long-time dream of his and it was finally coming true. He'd opened an office on Main Street for the project—complete with a model of the future resort in the waiting room—and hired a secretary. Thunder Canyon Ski Resort would be built on a ridge about twenty miles out of town on land the Douglases had owned for generations. Caleb had worked for months, hunting down investors. Everything had finally fallen into place in the past few weeks. Caleb had told her proudly that Justin's company, Red Rock Developers, was the main reason it was all working out.

"I think it's a solid investment," Justin said.

"Good for everyone, then."

"Yes. Absolutely."

Another silence descended. Oh, this was all so awkward. If she had to get herself stranded in a blizzard, you'd think it might have been with someone she knew. Or at least, maybe someone less…attractive.

He was almost too good-looking, really. And she felt a certain fluttery sensation in her midsection every time she glanced his way. Her excited response to him made her wary.

She wondered if he knew about her money. There *was* a lot of it. Katie mostly ignored it and let the estate managers handle everything. Her interests were in her family—and to her, that meant the Douglases—and in her town and in the Thunder Canyon Public Library, which she had generously endowed and where she was privileged to work at a job she truly loved.

But she could never completely forget that she was the sole heir to large fortunes on both her mother's and her father's side. Everybody in town knew it, of course. She'd even had a couple of boyfriends who'd turned out to be nothing more than fortune hunters in the end. From them she'd learned the hard truth: when it came to men, she had to be careful. If a man seemed interested, there was always a chance that his interest was more in her money than in Katie herself.

Sometimes she wished she could be like other women, and just go for it, when it came to guys. But she had a shy streak and she had too much money, and both made her more guarded than she would have liked to be.

She kept thinking of that kiss, back in the hall, kept remembering the feel of his mouth against hers....

But really, other than that kiss, which had only been for show, he'd made no moves on her. He wasn't even blaming her for the fact that they were stuck here for Lord knew how long.

She could have been stranded with worse, and she told herself firmly to remember that.

"Deep thoughts?" Justin asked softly.

"Not at all." She gestured at the trays of food. "If you've had all you want, I think we should go ahead and put this stuff away...."

He gave her a level look. She knew what he was thinking. They could very well end up enjoying those sandwiches for breakfast. "Let's do it." He rose and picked up a tray and the pitcher of grape drink.

She grabbed another tray and followed him through the main display room, to the kitchen at the back.

Twenty minutes later, they had everything put away. They returned to the reception room and sat down again. They made halting conversation. He told her a little about his company, said he'd started from nothing and had "come a long way."

"You're based in...?"

"Bozeman."

"Did you grow up in Montana?"

"No. I was born in California. We moved a lot. To Oregon for a while and later to Colorado, Nevada, Idaho..."

"Brothers and sisters?"

"Single mom—and she only had me. She died two years ago."

"It must have been tough for her...."

"Yeah. It was." He'd rested his dark head back against the knotty pine wall. He glanced her way. "We could use a television. Or at least a radio."

Boy, could they. "We can look around for one."

So they returned to the kitchen and went through the cabinets. Nothing but pots and pans and dishes and such. In the storage room off one of the side display rooms, where the society kept the donations they were collecting for their next rummage sale, they did find a battered old boom box.

Justin scanned the small room. "Any plugs in here?"

"Just the one in the light." They both looked up at the bare bulb above. The cord wouldn't stretch that far. "Why don't we take it with us out front?"

"Fine," he said, glancing around. "Lots of clothes in these bags…" They shared another look and she knew they were thinking along the same lines. If they didn't get out of here soon, they could always go through the bags, maybe find something more comfortable to wear.

The idea depressed her—that they might be stuck here long enough to need a change of clothes.

"Look at it this way," he advised gently. "We're safe and warm. And we've got plenty of sandwiches."

They took the radio out through the silent display rooms to the front. Justin plugged it in and turned the dial. Nothing but static.

Thoroughly discouraged, Katie went to the window

again. She wrapped her arms around herself and stared out for a while at the steadily falling snow.

Justin spoke from behind her. "Those old beds in the center display room..."

She faced him. They shared a grim look.

He asked, "Are you thinking what I'm thinking?"

Her nod was resigned. "It does begin to look as if they're going to get some use tonight."

Past midnight, Justin Caldwell lay wide-awake staring at the shadowed rafters in the museum's central room. He'd taken the narrow, hard little cot in the one-room pioneer cabin display and stretched out, fully clothed but for those damn too-small boots, under the star-patterned quilt. He'd had to pull out the sheet at the bottom of the bed. It was too short by a foot and his stocking feet hung out over the edge.

But at least the bedding was clean. Katie had told him it was all antique stuff donated by local families. The Historical Society took pains to keep it laundered and in good repair.

Katie...

He could hear her soft breathing from the "bedroom" on the opposite wall, where she lay in a wide four-poster with pineapple finials that some pioneer family had probably dragged across the plains in a covered wagon. He smiled to himself.

She was...a surprise. A quiet woman; self-contained. With those wide honey-brown eyes, that tender mouth and the shy way she had about her, she seemed, in some ways, so young—younger than her age, which he knew was twenty-four.

Yes. Very young. And yet, at the same time, she had that self-possessed quality that made her, somehow, seem older.

He knew much more than she'd told him so far. He'd paid and paid well to learn all about her—and about Caleb, Adele and Riley Douglas, as well.

Katherine Adele Fenton was the only child of the jet-setting Paris and Darrin Fenton. She'd been born in Venice, Italy—and immediately turned over to a nanny. Into her teens, Katie hardly saw her parents. She was fourteen and living a sheltered life with a governess in London when both Paris and Darrin died tragically; their private plane crashed on the way to a society wedding.

That was where the Douglases came in. As Katie's godmother, Adele had gone back east to claim the orphaned child of her dear college friend.

From what Justin had been able to learn, the Douglases considered Katie one of their own. She was, though not by blood, a full-fledged member of their family. She was the daughter Adele Douglas never had. Though he'd taken her into his home and treated her as family, Caleb had never made any effort to lay claim to a red cent of Katie's considerable inheritance. And from what Justin knew of Caleb Douglas—who loved nothing so much as making big deals involving large sums of money—that was saying something.

Justin pushed back the quilt. When he returned to the hard pallet laughingly called a bed, he'd leave off the blankets. The old building's heating system seemed to have one temperature: high. He sat and swung his legs soundlessly to the floor.

Rising, he ducked under the rope that was supposed to keep visitors away from the displays, and went to the door that led out to the reception area. It opened soundlessly and he shut it without letting the latch click.

In the men's room off the reception area, he flicked on the light and used the urinal. At the sink, he splashed cold water on his face and avoided meeting his own eyes in the mirror.

Back in the reception area, he stood by the window. The snow was still coming down. It lay, thick and white and sparkling, covering the steps up to porch level.

If it kept up like this, they could be stuck here for a day or two. Maybe longer. Who the hell knew?

Lots of time alone, just him and Katie…

Though he generally preferred a more outgoing, sophisticated type of woman, he *was* drawn to her. In the end, he supposed, there was no predicting sexual chemistry.

She felt attracted to him, too. He'd seen it in those big brown eyes of hers, known it in the way her body softened and melted into him during that kiss that had sealed their fake vows back there at the town hall.

Maybe he had something here. Maybe he ought to consider taking advantage of the way this sudden winter storm had thrown them together.

But he would have to watch himself. He couldn't let things get *too* hot and heavy. He had nothing with him to protect her from pregnancy and he'd have wagered half his assets that Katie Fenton wasn't on the pill.

No. He couldn't take the chance that she might become pregnant. He'd grown up without a father and he knew what that could do to a kid.

But he could certainly draw her out a little. No doubt she knew things about the Douglases—things that even his expert, high-priced sources couldn't have dug up. Knowledge *was* power and the more he had of it, the better his position would be in this special game he was playing.

And in spite of her wariness, Katie should be approachable if he took the right tact with her—if he were frank and friendly; helpful and easygoing…

It wouldn't have to go too far. Just enough for her to trust him, to tell him her secrets—and those of the Douglases. Just enough that she would *believe* in him as a man. Just enough that she'd come to…care for him.

In the end, if he worked it right, she'd be brokenhearted. He regretted that. But when it came time for payback, a man had to accept some degree of collateral damage. She would be hurt—and the people who cared most about her would hurt *for* her. It would add a certain…turn of the knife, you might say.

Justin flicked off the porch light. No need for it at this late hour. The window became a dark mirror. He saw his own reflection faintly, a lurking shadow in the glass.

Hell.

Maybe not.

He'd always been a man who did what needed doing. Still, he was having a little trouble getting around the fact that Katie Fenton was a good woman. An innocent in all this.

He should leave her out of it.

But then, if it worked out according to plan, he wouldn't be hurting her *that* bad. Just a little. Just enough to get to Caleb. She'd get over it in time.

And there was no saying that he could even fool her. She might be innocent, but she was also smart. It was just possible she'd see him coming and refuse to let him get close enough to make her care. They'd be locked in here for a day or two and she would merely tolerate him until their time of forced proximity had passed. She'd escape unscathed.

Maybe.

But then again, there *was* the real attraction between them. If he let himself go with that, he wouldn't be faking it. And he would tell her the truth—just not all of it.

Taking it forward from that angle…

Say it was all the same, except for the fact that she'd been raised by the Douglases. Say she was only the town librarian playing the mail-order bride and he'd been a stranger talked into taking the part of her groom. Say they ended up here, alone, snowed in at the museum, just as they had.

Take away her connection to the Douglases and he would still be intrigued with her, would still want to pursue her, to hear her secrets, to hold her in his arms and steal a kiss or two.

So in the end, he would only be doing what he

would have done, anyway: getting to know a woman who interested him.

Yes. He could look at it that way. He could take it from there and go with it. Be friendly and open and willing to talk about himself—to hear about her and her life and the people she cared for.

Maybe nothing would come of it.

Or maybe, in the end, he'd have found a second, more personal way to make Caleb Douglas pay for his sins.

## Chapter Three

Katie woke to the smell of coffee brewing.

That was the good news.

Everything else? Not nearly so pleasant. Her mouth tasted like the bottom of someone's old shoe. Her wrinkled wool dress gave off a distinctly musty odor. And she had a crick in her neck from sleeping on a too-fat pillow.

She let out a loud, grumpy groan—and then snapped her mouth shut. After all, there was a virtual stranger in the bed across the way—or wait. Probably not. He must be the one who'd made the coffee.

Katie sat up. She'd left the dimmer set to low, so the light was minimal, but she could see that Justin Caldwell's narrow cot lay empty, the covers pulled up and neatly tucked in.

Anxious, suddenly, to know what time it was, to

find out if the storm had ended, if it might be possible that she could go home to her own comfy house on Cedar Street, Katie threw back the covers and jumped from the old bed. Ducking under the rope that marked off her ''room,'' she pulled open the door to the reception area—and blinked at what she saw.

Beyond the windows, a wall of snow gleamed at her in the gray light of a cloud-thick Sunday morning. It was piled above the porch floor now. Though the wild winds of last night had died in the darkness, the snow itself continued to fall, a filmy white curtain, whispering its way down.

The clock on the wall read seven-fifteen. She picked up the phone. Silence. With a heavy sigh, she set it down again and headed for the ladies' room, where she used the facilities, rinsed her face and made a brave effort to comb her tangled hair with her fingers.

Snowed-in without even a hairbrush. Definitely not her idea of a good time.

In the kitchen, Katie found Justin sitting at the table by the window, wearing jeans and a cable-knit red and green sweater with reindeer leaping in a line across his broad chest. On his feet were a battered pair of black-and-white lace-up canvas All-Stars.

''It's true,'' he announced at her look. ''I have raided the rummage sale bags and I feel no shame.''

''Love the sweater,'' she muttered glumly. ''Phone's still dead.'' Beyond him, out the window, the snow kept coming down. ''They won't even be able to get the plow out in this.''

"Relax," he advised with an easy shrug. "Have some coffee." He toasted her with his stoneware mug. "I even found a smaller pot, so we don't have to brew it up for a hundred every time we want a cup." He gestured at the plateful of sandwiches on the table. "And did I mention there are plenty of sandwiches?"

"Wonderful." She padded to the counter, poured herself some coffee, added cream from the carton in the fridge and plunked herself down in the chair opposite him.

"Better?" he asked after she'd taken a sip.

"A little. Though I'd give a good number of stale sandwiches for a toothbrush. And a comb." She put a hand to her tangled hair. "If we're stuck here much longer, I may consider raiding the museum displays for some long-gone pioneer lady's sterling silver dresser set."

He looked very pleased with himself—and, now she thought about it, he looked as if he'd shaved. And his hair was wet—was that shampoo she smelled?

She set down her cup. "You found a razor in the rummage sale bags—and you washed your hair."

He laughed. It was a low, velvety kind of sound and it played along her skin like a physical caress. "Was that an accusation?"

She sat back in her chair and regarded him with suspicion. "You're much too cheerful."

"And you are very cranky." He took another bite of his sandwich, chewed and swallowed. "If you don't be nice, I won't let you have what's in that bag over by the sink."

She glanced where he'd indicated. The bag sat near the edge: a plain brown paper bag. "What's in it?"

He pushed the plate of sandwiches toward her. "Eat first."

She reached for a sandwich, raised it to her lips—and lowered it without taking a bite. "Just tell me. Is there a hairbrush in there?"

He nodded. "More than one. And combs. And a few toothbrushes—still wrapped in cellophane. And travel-size toothpaste. And sample bottles of shampoo and lotion, boxed-up shower caps and miniature bars of soap—oh, and did I mention razors and travel-size shaving cream cans? Looks like someone held up a drugstore, raided a motel supply closet and gave what they stole to the Historical Society rummage sale."

"Shower caps," Katie repeated wistfully.

Justin grunted. "Yeah. No need for those."

"Since we don't have a shower."

"But remember. It could be worse. The heat could be out and there could be no wood for the stove. The ladies from the Historical Society could have failed to leave us these delicious sandwiches." He waved one at her.

"You have a surprisingly vivid imagination."

"Thank you. And what I meant is, we're doing okay here. And after you eat, you even get to brush your teeth."

She supposed he had a point. "You're right. I should take my own advice from yesterday and keep a more positive outlook on our situation."

He faked a stern expression. "See that you do."

Katie ate her sandwich and took a second, as well.

Her spirits had lifted. If she wasn't getting out of here today, at least she'd have clean teeth and combed hair.

Once she'd spent twenty minutes in the ladies' room using various items from the brown paper bag, Katie went to the storage area and chose a bulky sweater and a pair of worn corduroy pants. She even found thick gray socks and jogging shoes that were only a half size too big.

"Lookin' good," Justin remarked with a wink when she returned to the kitchen where he sat reading yesterday's newspaper.

"The fit leaves something to be desired—but I have to admit, I'm a lot more comfortable."

"And less cranky."

"Yes. That, too." She gave him a smile, thinking how even-tempered and helpful he'd been since she got them into this mess. Really, she could have been stranded with worse. She added, in an effort to show him her friendlier side, "While I was choosing my outfit, I found some old board games. Maybe we can haul them out later. I play a mean game of checkers."

"Sounds good." The paper rustled as he turned the page.

"Justin…"

He lowered the paper and gave her an easy smile.

"I just want you to know I appreciate how well you're taking all this."

He gestured toward the snow beyond the window. "This is nothing, believe me."

Really, this positive-attitude approach could be carried too far. "Oh. So you're telling me this kind of thing happens to you all the time?"

"Only once before."

"Oh. Well. Only once. That's nothing—and you're joking, aren't you?"

"No. I'm not. When I was thirteen, we lived in this vacation-home development in northern Nevada. I got snowed-in there alone for a week."

She couldn't have heard right. "Alone for a week—at thirteen?" He nodded. "But what about your mom?"

"She was supposed to be home, but she didn't make it. The situation was similar to yesterday's—a sudden storm that turned out much worse than predicted. It got bad fast and she couldn't get to me."

"But…where was she?"

His expression turned doubtful. "You sure you want to hear this? It's not that exciting. And as you can see by looking at me today, I got through it just fine."

She'd been planning to go check on Buttercup. But that could wait a minute or two. She pulled out a chair and slid into it. "I do want to hear. Honestly."

He studied her for a long moment, as if gauging the sincerity of her request. Finally, he folded the paper and set it aside. "At the time, we were living in this one-room cabin not far from Lake Tahoe."

"You and your mom?"

"That's right. The cabin was one of those ski chalet designs. On a two-acre lot. Intended as a vacation home. It had a single big, open room with lots of windows, the roof pitched high, a sleeping loft above?''

''Yes. I can picture it.''

''My mother was in real estate at that point. She went off to show someone another cabin identical to ours. A bad storm blew in. She couldn't get back to me, so I was stuck on my own. It was…a learning experience, let me tell you.''

''Yikes. I can't even imagine.''

''Yeah. It *was* pretty grim, looking back on it. The phone line went dead the first day. Then, the next day, the power went out. But I had plenty of candles and a woodstove for heat. I kept the fire going and tucked into the canned goods when I got hungry.''

''But what did you *do,* alone for all that time?''

One corner of his full mouth quirked up. ''I got pretty damn bored, now you mention it. Bored enough that I taught myself solitaire with a dog-eared deck of cards I found in a kitchen drawer. When that got old, I started working my way through all my schoolbooks. For a thirteen-year-old boy to do every problem in his math book for recreation, *that's* desperation.''

''But there was plenty of canned food, you said?''

He made a low sound in his throat. ''For some reason, my mom had a case each of canned peaches and cream of mushroom soup. To this day, I can't stand the sight or smell of either.''

''I'll bet—but what I can't imagine is how you made it through something like that.'' She scanned his face. ''Thirteen,'' she said softly. ''It's too horrible. You must have been scared to death.''

He shrugged. "The wood lasted 'til the end of the sixth day. I got out the axe and chopped up my mother's oak-veneer kitchen table and chairs. Once I'd burned them, I kind of lost heart. The fire died and I piled every blanket in the place on my bed and burrowed in there for the duration. I have to admit, by that time I was getting pretty damn terrified."

"But then you were rescued."

"That's right. The snowplow arrived at noon the next day with my mother, in her Blazer, right behind it. She was seriously freaked, I can tell you."

Katie almost wished his mother could have been there, with them, right then. She'd have had a thing or two to say to her. "Your *mother* was freaked. What about you? *You* were the child, for heaven's sake. How could she leave you alone like that?"

He let out a low chuckle. "Katie. Settle down."

Easier said than done. His story had seriously hit home for her. She shifted in her chair, crossing her legs and then uncrossing them, feeling antsy and angry and definitely not *settled down.* "I'm sorry, but it just, well, it fries me, you know? Children are so vulnerable. Parents have to look out for them, take *care* of them, pay them some attention now and then...."

He sat back in his chair. "Why do I get the feeling you're talking about more than what happened to me when I was thirteen?"

She wrapped her arms around her middle and looked out the window at the falling snow, blinking against the glare of all that shimmery white.

"Katie?"

She faced him. "You're right," she confessed. "I was thinking about how things were for me, before Addy came and got me, when my parents were still alive."

"Rough?" Those blue eyes had a softness in them, as if he understood—and from what he'd just told her, she had a feeling he did.

She hugged herself harder. "I rarely saw them. They enjoyed traveling. They had a flat in London, the family brownstone in Philadelphia, villas in France and Italy. And where they didn't have a flat or a villa, they had *friends* who had one. You know the words. 'Globe-trotting.' 'Jet-setting.' My parents *were* the beautiful people. They came from fine families and the money was always there. They never had to work. So they didn't. They didn't even have to take care of their child. There were nannies and governesses, plenty of hired help for that."

"So you weren't left alone," Justin said, his eyes direct. Knowing.

"No, I wasn't."

"But you *were* lonely."

"Exactly." She looked down. Her arms were wrapped so tightly around her middle, they made her rib cage ache. With a slow, deep breath, she let go of herself and folded her hands on the tabletop. "I never knew a real family—'til Addy and Caleb." She smiled to herself. "And Riley. He was all grown up by the time I came to them, twenty-three, when I moved to the ranch. How many young guys in their twenties have time for a gawky fourteen-year-old girl? Not many. But Riley did. He was so good to me, you know?'' Justin made a sound of understanding low in his throat. "What the Douglases gave me was something so important. The two big things I'd never had. Their time. Their attention. Riley taught me to ride—''

"On Buttercup." He grinned.

"That's right." She glanced toward the door to the back porch, thinking she should get out there and check on the old mare. Soon.

But it was so…comfortable. Sitting here with Justin, talking about the things that had made them who they were. "So you don't blame your mother for leaving you alone in that cabin?"

He shook his head. "It's tough for a woman on her own, with a kid. She'd been left high and dry, pregnant with me by the no-good bastard who used her and then walked away from her when she told him she was having his baby. She was…a good mother and she took damn good care of me. But there was no getting around that she had to make a living and that meant when the storm blew in, I was at the cabin, and she wasn't. It's the kind of thing that can happen to anyone.''

"It's the kind of thing that could scar a child for life, that's what it is.''

He pressed a fist to his chest right over the row of reindeer prancing across the front of his sweater. "That's me. Deeply damaged.''

She tipped her head to the side, considering. "Well. I guess it's good that you can joke about it.''

He was quiet for a moment. Then he said, "It happened. I survived. And I've done just fine for myself, though I never had a father, never had much formal education and started, literally, from scratch.''

"In...development?'' She laughed. "What does that mean, exactly, to be a 'developer.'''

"Well, a developer 'develops.'''

"Sheesh. It's all clear to me now.''

He grinned. "Property, in my case. We start with several viable acres and we develop a project to build tract homes. Or say I got hold of just the right business-district lot. I'd start putting the people and financing together to build an office complex. A developer is someone who gets the money and the people and the plans—and most important, the right property—and puts it all together.''

He hadn't told her anything she couldn't have figured out herself, but she was discovering she enjoyed listening to him talk. She liked the way he looked at her. As if he never wanted to look away.

She said, "Like Caleb's ski resort? He's got the property and you'll work with him to 'develop' it.''

"That's right. But don't misunderstand. It's his project, his baby. He'll be in charge, though I'll be involved every step of the way.''

She looked down at her folded hands. She was just about to tell him how much the project meant to Caleb. Caleb *was* getting older and Katie knew that sometimes he worried he was losing his edge—but no.

Katie kept her mouth shut. Yes, she was finding she liked Justin. A lot. However, the last thing Caleb would want was for her to go blabbing his secret doubts to a business associate.

She glanced up and found Justin studying her again, his dark head tipped to the side. "Question."

"Ask."

"Yesterday. Didn't you mention that you went to college in Colorado?"

"That's right. CU."

"I'll bet you had straight A's in high school."

She gave him a pert little nod. "You would win that bet."

"High scores on the SAT?"

"Very."

"Then why not Bryn Mawr, like your mother, and Adele Douglas? You'd have been a legacy, right— pretty much guaranteed to get in—even if your grades and test scores hadn't been outstanding?"

"I liked CU. They have a fine curriculum. Plus, it was closer to home."

"Home being here, in Thunder Canyon."

"That's right—and you? Where did you go to college?"

"I told you. No real formal education. I went to real estate school and then got my broker's license a couple of years later."

"You started in real estate because of your mother's connections?"

He chuckled at that, though there wasn't a lot of humor in the sound. "My mother had no connections. She'd been out of the real estate business for years when I started. It didn't work out for her. Like a lot of things…"

She might have asked, *What things?* But he wore a closed-in, private kind of look at that moment and she didn't want to pry. She coaxed, "So you started in real estate…"

He blinked and the brooding shadows left his eyes. "Yeah. By the time I was twenty-five, I'd branched into property development."

"A self-made man."

"Smile when you say that."

She *was* smiling. But to make sure he noticed, she smiled even wider. And then her conscience reminded her that she had Buttercup to think of. She stood.

He put on a hurt look. "Just like that. You're leaving. Was it something I said?"

"What you said was fascinating. Honestly. And I'll be back soon."

"The question is, where do you think you're going?" He tipped his head toward the window and the still-falling snow outside. "I hate to break it to you, but I doubt you could get beyond the front porch."

"I want to check on Buttercup."

He rose. "I'll come with you."

She started to argue—that it was cold out there and she could take care of the job herself and he didn't really need to go. But then again, it wasn't as if he had a full schedule or anything.

He ushered her out to the back porch, where they put on their antique outerwear. Then they pushed open the door to the breezeway.

The snow had piled four feet or so on either side, sloping to the icy ground, leaving a path maybe a foot wide. "After you," Justin said. "Watch your step. It looks pretty slick."

In the shed, Buttercup snorted in greeting and came

right to Katie. She stroked the old mare's forehead and blew in her nostrils. "How're you doing, sweetie? Kind of lonely out here?" The horse whickered in response. "And I'll bet you wish I had some oats. Sorry. That hay'll have to do you for a while." She patted Buttercup's smooth golden neck and pulled out one of the brushes she'd brought from inside. It was hardly a grooming brush, but nothing else was available.

She brushed the old mare's knotted mane and spoke to her in low whispers for a while. Then she and Justin broke open another bale of hay.

"Watch out," he warned when they were spreading it around a little. "It's damned amazing how much manure one horse can produce in a sixteen-hour period."

"It is at that."

"Just don't step backward without looking behind you first."

She found a shovel in the corner and took it to him. "Get to work."

"Shoveling horse manure?"

"That's right."

"But where am I going to put it?" The gleam in his eyes said he already had a pretty good idea.

"Just shovel it up, carry it out those open main doors there and toss it as far as you can into the snow."

"That snow's piling up pretty high out there. This could be dangerous."

"So pay attention when you throw it. Wouldn't want it to come flying right back at you."

He pretended to grumble, but he started right in. She looked around and found another shovel. With both of them scooping and tossing, they had the mess cleared away in no time at all.

As they went to put the shovels up, Justin remarked that if the snow got much higher, swamping out the shed was going to be a real challenge.

"We'll manage," she told him. "Somehow…" She set her shovel against the wall and turned so fast, she almost ran into him.

"Watch it." He laughed down low in his throat, the sound emerging on a cloud of mist.

She laughed, too.

And then, all at once, she wasn't laughing and neither was he. They were just looking at each other—staring, really. And the cold air seemed to shimmer between them.

Oh, my goodness. Those lips of his…

Too full, for a man's lips. Really. Too full and yet…

Exactly perfect.

If only she didn't already know how delicious those lips felt pressed against her own. Maybe, if she didn't know what a great kisser he was, she wouldn't be standing here, sighing out a big breath of misty air and lifting her mouth to him.

He said her name, on a fog of breath. "Katie…"

She was so busy imagining what it was going to feel like when his lips met hers, that she didn't register how close Buttercup was behind him—not until the mare let out a low whinny and head-butted Justin a good one.

"Hey!" He surged forward, right into Katie. She went over backward and down they went into the newly spread hay. He ended up on top of her.

Katie blinked up at him and he looked down at her and there was a lovely, strange, breath-held kind of moment. He was so…warm and solid, pressed all along the length of her—and heavy, too, but in a good way. He looked deep in her eyes and he said her name again and she held up her lips to welcome his kiss.

But Buttercup wasn't finished. She bent her head and started nipping the back of Justin's baggy old coat.

He rolled away from Katie to glare up at the mare. "Knock it off."

Buttercup whinnied again and clopped off toward the double doors. A moment later, she was outside beneath the overhang, lipping up snow.

Justin canted up on an elbow and looked down at Katie. "That animal has it in for me."

Katie was thinking that she really ought to sit up. Her hat had come off when Justin landed on top of her. She knew she had hay in her hair. But she felt kind of…lax. Lax and lazy and oh-so-comfortable, lying there in the hay on the frozen dirt floor.

"Hmm," she said, and the sound was every bit as low and lazy as she was feeling. "Maybe Buttercup thinks you're up to no good."

He leaned in closer. She gazed up at his thick black lashes and his red nose and that wonderful, soft, oh-so-kissable mouth. "I'm perfectly harmless."

"Perfect?" she heard herself answer, her tone as

husky and intimate as his. "Maybe. Harmless? Oh, I don't think so...."

There was a silence, a quiet so intense she could hear the soft sound of the snow falling outside and the faint rustling noises Buttercup made beyond the shed doors. Slowly, his mouth curved into a smile. And his eyes...

Oh, it was just like right before he kissed her, in front of everyone, back in the hall. His eyes kind of sucked on her. They drew her down.

"I don't think that mare wants me to kiss you."

And she probably *shouldn't* kiss him. "Well, Justin. Okay, then. Let me up and we'll—"

He cut her off by placing a gloved finger against her lips. "Not yet." She probably should have protested, told him firmly to let her up.

But she didn't. She watched, entranced, as he lifted his hand, took the tip of the glove's finger between his white teeth and pulled it off. He dropped the glove beside her and then he touched her lips again—skin to skin this time. That brush of a caress made her mouth tingle, made her whole body yearn.

He let his hand drift over until it lay against the side of her face. "Soft," he whispered. "So pretty and soft..." He lowered his mouth.

She expected a hot, soul-shattering kiss. But he only brushed his lips sweetly, one time, across hers—and then he lifted away again and she was looking in those haunting eyes once more. "What's another kiss? Between a man and his wife."

Now she felt truly torn. She longed to kiss him—yet she knew it was probably a bad idea. "We shouldn't…get anything started, you know? We hardly know each other and—''

"But that's just it. I *want* to know you better. What about you, Katie? Do you want to know me?''

She did! And that seemed…dangerous, somehow. That seemed foolish and scary and simply not right. "I—I don't really want to start anything *casual,* you know?'' She found her throat had gone desert-dry. She paused to swallow and then rushed to continue before he could do anything that would make her thoughts scatter and fly away. "I know it's probably every guy's fantasy to get stranded with a woman who, uh, knows what she wants and knows how to get it—not that I don't know what I want. It's just, well, I don't want…*that.*''

He only smiled. "*That,* huh?''

"Yes.''

"That…what?''

Oh, this wasn't going well. "Look. I just don't want to start anything I know I'm not going to finish. Okay?''

"Katie?''

She glared at him. "What?''

"It's only a kiss.''

"Oh, I just don't—''

"Katie. Do you *want* to kiss me?''

"We've just about talked this to death, don't you think?''

"But do you want to kiss me?''

"Oh, all right, damn it.'' Katie rarely swore. But right then, *damn it* seemed the only thing to say.

"But do you?''

"Yes." The word came out breathless-sounding. "I do."

"Good." He lowered his mouth to hers.

Katie sighed once and she sighed again.

Her hands slipped up to encircle his neck and she held on for dear life as he played with her mouth. With that clever tongue of his, he traced the seam where her lips met, teasingly at first and then with a more insistent pressure. She couldn't resist him—didn't *want* to resist him. Shyly, she let her lips relax and he swept that tongue of his inside.

It was a shocking, thrilling thing, the way Justin Caldwell could use that mouth of his. And it was a truly wonderful thing, the way his body felt, so warm and close, pressed against her side, the way he smelled of soap and shaving cream.

His cold nose touched hers and his hot breath burned her icy cheek. As he kissed her, he stroked her with his hands. That was wonderful, too. Each separate caress left a burning trail of longing in its wake. He wrapped his arms around her and rolled a little, so they were both on their sides, and his hand moved lower, to the small of her back. He rubbed there, a sweet, firm pressure, soothing muscles cramped from sleeping on that lumpy ancient mattress last night.

She moaned and pressed herself all the tighter against him. His hand swept lower. He cupped her bottom and tucked her up into him.

That was when she felt the hard ridge in his jeans.

Oh, my.

Time to stop.

Time to stop right *now*.

She braced her hands on his shoulders and tore her mouth away from his. "That's enough." She looked at his face and she feared…

What?

She realized she didn't know. Her fear was formless, and yet she did feel it.

*Remember the others,* she reminded herself. *They were after your money. They hurt you. He could so easily do the same.…*

But even as she thought of that, she didn't believe it. Oh, he might hurt her, yes. But in her heart, she simply didn't believe it would be for her money.

Which probably made her the biggest fool in Montana.

He loosened his hold on her. With a deep sigh, he pressed his forehead to hers. "You're right," he said. "Enough."

She slid her hands down to his hard chest. Beneath her palms, she could feel his heat, and his heart racing. His breath came out in ragged puffs—just like hers.

She whispered, "We'd better go in."

He touched her hair. She thought that she'd never felt anything quite so lovely in her whole life as that—the tender caress of his hand on her hair. He threaded his chilled bare fingers up under the tangled strands and cupped the back of her neck. She took his cue and tipped her head up to look at him.

"Yeah," he said. His mouth was swollen from what he'd been doing to her, his eyes twin blue flames. "We'll go in. Now." He pressed one more quick, hard kiss on her lips—as if he realized he shouldn't, but couldn't resist. Her mouth burned at the contact.

Then he reached across her to grab his discarded glove. Rolling away from her, he rose. She scuttled to a sitting position.

"Here," he said.

She stared at his outstretched hand. It seemed…too dangerous to take it.

Her gaze tracked upward, to his face. She knew by the heated look in his eyes that if she reached out, he would only pull her close and start kissing her again—and the thrumming of her blood through her body left her no doubt that she would end up kissing him right back.

No. Not going to happen. She'd known this man less than twenty-four hours. And she refused to end up rolling around naked with him on a bed of hay in a freezing old shed.

"I can manage, thanks." She pulled off a glove and felt in her hair. It was just as she'd suspected: threaded through with bits of hay. "Oh, just look at me…."

Justin let his hand drop to his side. "I am." His voice was husky and low. And in his eyes she saw desire—*real* desire. For her.

And not only desire, but also something dark and lonely, something that might have been regret.

Katie's mouth went dust-dry. *This* was danger—a danger far beyond any threat a mere fortune hunter might pose. Peril to her tender heart, to her very soul.

No doubt about it. She wanted him—with a kind

of bone-melting yearning, with a merciless desire the like of which she'd never known before.

It was…a physical aching. A hunger in the blood.

Oh, she would have to watch herself with him. She would have to exercise a little caution, or she'd be in way over her head.

Somewhere far back in her mind, a taunting voice whispered, *Katie. Come on. You're already over your head. Over your head and falling fast.…*

## Chapter Four

*He shouldn't have kissed her.*

It had been a major error in judgment and Justin damn well knew that it had.

He shouldn't have kissed her. Not so soon, anyway—and certainly not in a prickly bed of hay on the frozen dirt floor of the shed out back, with that irritating old mare looking on.

Getting hot and heavy so fast had spooked her. She had her guard up and now he couldn't get past it.

They spent the rest of the endless day playing checkers, watching the snow fall, stoking the fire in the stove out front and reading books and magazines they found stacked in the storage room. Whenever they spoke, she made sure it was in polite generalities.

The snow kept falling. The radio played only static. And the phone stayed dead.

Justin could have kicked himself with his rummage sale Converse All-Star. The big loss of ground with her was his own damn fault. He'd sucked her in beautifully, had her right in the palm of his hand once he'd told her the story of that lonely week in the cabin when he was thirteen. He'd hit the perfect common nerve: a lonely childhood; parents who weren't all they should have been.

It was going so well.

Until the kiss.

And even that could have been okay—could have been tender and sweet and worked beautifully to lure her closer.

But he'd gotten his arms around her and her mouth under his and that sweet body pressed close against him...

He'd lost it. Lost every last shred of control.

The bald truth was that he'd seriously underestimated the power of his own lust for the shy brown-eyed librarian with too much money and an adopted family he despised.

It was funny, really—though he wasn't laughing. A royal backfire of his basic intention: *he* was supposed to seduce *her*.

Not the other way around.

At six that evening, they sat at the kitchen table, reading—or at least, Katie was reading. He knew it because he kept sneaking glances at her and losing his place in the thriller that should have been holding him spellbound—or so it said in the cover notes. As "taut" and "edge-of-your seat" as the book was supposed to be, he kept having to go back and read the same paragraph over and over again.

Katie, though…

She seemed to have no trouble at all with her concentration. She'd laid the heavy volume she'd chosen open on the table, rested her forearms on the tabletop and bent her brown head to the page. She'd barely budged from that position for over an hour. He knew. He'd timed her. Occasionally, she'd catch her soft bottom lip between her teeth, worry it lightly and let it go. Sometimes she smiled—just the faintest hint of a smile. As if what she read amused her.

Justin scowled every time she smiled like that. He wanted her to look up and smile at *him,* damn it. But she didn't.

And he ought to be glad she didn't look up. If she caught him scowling at her, he'd only lose more ground than he already had.

And what the hell was his problem here, anyway? He was getting way too invested in this thing with her. She had nothing to do with the main plan and if she never let him get near her again it wouldn't matter in the least.

So why should he care if she smiled at him or not?

He decided he'd be better off not thinking too deeply on that one.

Luckily for him, he'd just looked down at his book again when she glanced up and announced, ''You know, when we went through the cupboards in here yesterday, I noticed some cans way in the back.''

There was something in her tone—something easier, a little more friendly.

His pulse ratcheted up a notch and he quelled a satisfied smile. *Better,* he thought. *Now, don't blow it....*

He shut the battered paperback without marking the page. Next time he picked it up, he'd have to start over, anyway. "Yeah," he said, sounding a hell of a lot more offhand than he felt. He gestured toward the cabinets on the far wall. "In the bottom, on the left." He started to rise.

"No. I'll look."

He sank back to his seat and she got up and went over there, leaving him debating whether to follow her. He decided against it. She *was* loosening up a little. Better let her get looser before he got too close.

She went to knees, pulled open the cupboard and stuck her head in there. He looked at her backside. Great view. Even with the ugly baggy sweater and too-loose frayed corduroy pants.

"Yes," she said, her voice muffled by the cabinet. "Here they are." She pulled her head out and craned around to grin at him. "Lots of soup, but I see some canned fruit, too."

He got up, after all, and went to stand over her—just to be helpful. She passed him the dusty cans and he set them on the counter above the cabinet.

"That's it." She shut the cabinet doors and stood to read the labels. "Vegetable beef, chicken noodle, cream of asparagus, pears, applesauce..." She gave him a pert look. "Justin. Not a single can of cream of mushroom soup. And no peaches."

Absurdly pleased that she'd remembered the details of his childhood ordeal, he allowed himself to chuckle. "That's a relief. I admit I was getting worried."

"No need to." She brushed his arm—the lightest breath of a touch. Beneath the green sleeve of his sweater, his skin burned as if she'd set a match to it.

Their eyes met. *Zap.* His heart raced faster and the air seemed to shimmer around them. Damned amazing, her effect on him.

Katie smiled wider, a nervous kind of smile. Yes. She *was* trying. She wasn't cutting him out anymore. "So...soup with your sandwiches?"

He nodded. "Vegetable beef—unless that's your favorite?"

She admitted, "I have this thing for cream of asparagus."

"Well, then. Looks like we both get what we want."

Katie went to get ready for bed at ten. Justin said he wanted to read a little longer and then he'd be in.

She knew it was only a pretense. In the hours they'd sat reading, he'd hardly made it through the first few chapters in that book of his. No. He was being thoughtful, giving her a chance to get ready and go to bed in private.

In the ladies' room, she rinsed out her underwear and hung it over the stall door. She washed up and dressed for bed in a wrinkled old pair of red flannel pajamas—thanks, again, to the bags of clothing in the storage room.

She looked at herself in the mirror over the sink and scrunched up her nose at what she saw. Tomorrow, if they were still stuck here, she would have to wash her hair. Maybe she could find some bath towels in the rummage sale stuff—or if not, well, she'd work it out somehow. And really, Justin didn't need to be sitting in the kitchen pretending to read, respecting her need to keep her distance from him after the kiss that had gone too far out in the shed.

"Stupid," she muttered to her own reflection. "I'm being stupid about this and I need to stop." There was nothing alluring or lust-inspiring about the sight of her in flannel pajamas. They buttoned up to here and bagged around her ankles. If Justin saw her getting into bed in them he would not be the least tempted to make mad, passionate love to her.

Truly. In pajamas like these, she was safe from the potential to have sex of any kind.

She peered closer at herself, craned her head forward so her nose met the glass. The question was, why did that depress her?

Oh, come on. She knew why.

Because there had not been nearly enough sex—of any kind—in her life.

"I, Katherine Adele Fenton," she whispered, her breath fogging the glass, "am a cliché. I'm right out of *The Music Man*. I'm Marian the librarian—hiding in the stacks, waiting for some cocky con man to show up and let down my hair for me."

Really, it had to stop. She owed it to librarians everywhere, who, she knew, were a much more outgoing, ready-for-anything bunch than most people gave them credit for.

She pulled back from the mirror and then used her

flannel sleeve to wipe the steamed-up place her breath had left. She stood straight and proud. "I *wanted* him to kiss me and I'm *glad* he kissed me," she announced to the sink and the toilet stall and her soggy underwear hanging from the stall door. "I'm not afraid of my own feelings. I'm an adult and I run my own life and I do it very well, thank you." She *liked* Justin and he clearly liked her and she wasn't running away from that. Not anymore.

Yes, there was always danger—when you really liked someone, when you put your heart on the line. Things that mattered inevitably involved a certain amount of risk.

Her shoulders back and her head high, Katie marched to the ladies' room door and pulled it wide.

Justin looked up from his book when she entered the kitchen. The bewildered expression on his handsome face made her want to grab him and hug him and tell him it would be all right. She didn't, of course. There were a few things that needed saying before they got around to any hugging.

"Katie? Everything okay?"

She marched over, yanked out the chair opposite him and dropped into it. "It was very sweet of you, to sit in here with that book you're not really interested in and wait until I had time to put on these ugly old pajamas and get into bed. But it's not as if we had to share a bathroom or anything." She raised her arms and looked down at her baggy bedroom attire. "And as you can see, this outfit reveals absolutely nothing of my, er, feminine charms. We're both perfectly safe from any, um, dangerous temptation, don't you think?'' She lifted her head and met his eyes.

They were gleaming. ''Well, Katie. I don't know. You look pretty damn tempting to me.''

''Liar,'' she muttered, flattered in spite of herself.

He put up a hand, palm out, as if testifying in court. ''Sexiest woman I ever saw.''

''Oh, yeah, right.''

''Must be the color. You know what they say about red. The color of power. And sex.''

She sat up straighter. ''Power, huh? I kind of like that.''

In his eyes she could see what he almost said: *But what about sex?* He didn't, though.

Probably afraid she'd get spooked and shut him out again.

''Justin?'' Her heart pounded painfully inside her rib cage. She had things to say and she was going to say them, but that didn't make it easy.

''Yeah?''

''Justin, are you after my money?''

With zero hesitation, he replied, ''No.''

She peered at him through narrowed eyes. ''Are you *sure*?''

''Yeah. Money's not an issue for me. I have plenty of my own. Now, anyway. And I earned every damn penny of it.''

Her face felt as if it had turned as red as her pajamas and her heart beat even faster. She did believe him. If that made her a total fool, well, so be it.

He added, ''But don't take me wrong. I don't mind

that you're rich. Hey, I'm glad you are. It's always better, don't you think, to have money than not to?''

Katie thought about that. ''Sometimes I'm not so sure. Money can…isolate a person. It can make it so it's hard to believe that someone might like you, just for yourself.''

''Katie.''

She put her hand against her heart. Really, did it need to keep pounding so awfully fast? ''Yeah?''

''I do like you. For yourself.''

She realized she believed that, too, and her galloping heart slowed a little. But she wasn't finished yet. ''There's more.''

''Shoot.''

''Did you know that I was…?'' Oh, this was so awkward.

He helped her out. ''Rich?''

She gulped. ''Yes. Did you know I was a wealthy woman before you got up on that stage at the town hall and 'married' me?''

''I did.''

She blinked. ''Who told you?''

He chuckled. ''Some of those spectators were pretty damn drunk. When they heard I'd be playing your groom, I got a lot of ribbing. You know the kind. How you were not only a cute little thing, you were loaded, too. How, if I played my cards right, I might catch myself an heiress.''

Katie scrunched up her nose. ''A cute little thing?''

He shrugged. ''Drunk talk. You know how it goes. And you might like to know, I got more than one warning that I'd better be good to you. They were joking—but the look in every eye said I'd pay if I messed with their favorite librarian.''

That brought a smile. ''They did? They told you to be good to me?''

He nodded. ''So you've got backup, in case you were worried.''

She looked him directly in the eye. ''I guess I *was* worried. And scared. The truth is, in the past couple of years, I've had a tendency to let fear run my life. But I've had a little talk with myself. Fear is not going to rule me. Not anymore. I…well, I like you. And I think you like me.''

''I do. Very much.''

A sweet warmth spread through her. ''So then. I'd like to get to know you better.''

His gaze didn't waver. ''And I want to know you.''

## Chapter Five

They talked for hours, lying in their separate beds in the central display room.

Katie told him about Ted Anders. She'd met Ted at CU. He was tall and tan and blond, a prelaw student. Interesting to talk to, with a good sense of humor—and charming, too. Extremely so. Ted had lavished attention on Katie. She'd started to believe she'd found the right guy for her—until she went to a party up on "the hill," where a lot of the students shared apartments. The place was packed, a real crowd scene. She got separated from Ted and when she found him again, he had his arm around a cute redhead.

"He was so busy putting a move on her, he didn't even see that I was watching," Katie said. "I heard him tell her how he'd like to, uh, 'jump her bones,' but he couldn't afford to. He had a 'rich one' on a string and he wasn't blowing that 'til he'd clipped at least a couple of her millions.''

"I hope you reamed him a new one right there and then." Justin sounded as if he wouldn't have minded doing that for her.

She laughed—and it felt so good. To think about something that had hurt so much at the time and re-alize it was just a memory now, one with no power to cause her pain. "In case you didn't notice, I'm not big on public displays."

He chuckled. "Well, yeah. As a matter of fact, I did notice. So, what *did* you do?"

"I went home to my apartment. Eventually, Ted must have realized I'd left. He came knocking on my door. I confronted him then. He started laying on the sweet talk. But I wasn't buying. Once he saw he couldn't talk his way back into a relationship with me, he said a few rotten things, trying to hurt me a little worse than he already had. But he knew it was over."

"And that made you sure every man you met would be after your money?"

"Well, there was another, er, incident."

"At CU?"

"No. Right here in town, not long after I came home to stay and took the job as librarian. He was a local guy, Jackson Tully. He'd grown up here and gone to Thunder Canyon High ten years before I did. After high school, he'd moved away—and then moved back and opened a souvenir shop on Main. He asked me out and he seemed nice enough. We had several dates and…oh, he was funny and sweet and I started to think—"

"That he was *the one*."

She made a face at the shadowed rafters above. "Oh, I don't know. I thought that we had something good, I guess. That it might really go somewhere."

"As in wedding bells and happily ever after?"

"That's right."

"So then…?"

"Well, he proposed."

"Marriage?"

"What else?"

He made a low sound. "I can think of a few other things, but I won't go into them. So the money-grubbing shop owner proposed and you said yes."

She pushed the blankets down a little and rested her arms on top of them. "Well, no. I didn't say yes. I did…care for him, but I wasn't sure. I said I wanted to think about it. And while I was thinking, his mom came to see me. She's a nice woman, Lucille Tully is. A member of the Historical Society, as a matter of fact."

"Isn't everyone?"

"In Thunder Canyon?" She considered. "Well, just about everyone over forty or so is."

"And Lucille Tully said…"

"That she loved her son, but I was a 'sweet girl' and she couldn't let me say yes to him without my knowing the truth."

"Which was?"

"Jackson had had two bankruptcies. His souvenir shop—which Lucille had given him the money to open—wasn't doing well and he'd told his mother more than once that as soon as he married the librarian, she could have her money back. He'd close the store. Why slave all day long, catering to pushy tourists in some stupid shop when he'd be set for life and he could focus on enjoying himself.''

"Spending your money, I take it?"

Katie sighed. "Lucille cried when she told me. I felt terrible for her. It just broke her heart, the whole thing."

"So you said no to the gold-digging Jackson Tully."

"I did."

"And where is he now?"

"Couldn't say. His shop went under and he left town. So far as I know, he hasn't been back."

"And what about the mother?"

"What do you mean?"

"Come on, Katie. I've known you for two whole days and I can already guarantee that you took care of her."

"Well, if you must know, I had Caleb buy the shop."

"With *your* money."

"That's right. Caleb made sure Jackson paid Lucille back. Then Caleb sold the shop for me. At a profit. Everybody came out all right—financially, at least. And by then, Jackson had moved on. Lucille doesn't talk about him much, not to me, anyway— and you know, now I look back on both Jackson and Ted Anders, I realize I was pretty darn lucky. At least I didn't marry them. At least I found out what kind of men they really were before I took any kind of irrevocable step.''

There was silence from the narrow cot on the other side of the room.

She grinned into the darkness. ''Justin? Have I put you to sleep?''

''I'm wide-awake.''

''You sound so serious…''

A pause, and then, ''Those two were a couple of prime-grade SOBs—and you're right, at least you didn't marry either of them.''

''No, I didn't. And Justin…''

''What?''

''I did have a *nice* boyfriend or two. Nothing that serious, but they were good guys. I actually enjoyed high school. How many people can say that?''

''Good point.'' The way he said that made her sure he was one of the ones who couldn't.

''And I went to both proms—junior and senior. For my senior prom I wore a—''

He made a loud snoring sound.

She sat up and the bed creaked in protest. ''I might have to unscrew one of these pineapple finials and throw it at you.''

He sat up, too. ''Please don't hurt me.''

They looked at each other through the darkness. For pajamas, he'd found a pair of cheap black sweats in the storage room. In the minimal light, he was hardly more than a broad-shouldered shadow. But then his white teeth flashed with his smile.

She flopped back down. ''I promise to let you go to sleep. Soon.''

His blankets rustled. "No hurry. As it happens, I don't have any early appointments tomorrow."

"Okay, then. But remember. I offered to shut up...."

"And I turned you down."

She raised her arms and slid her hands under her hair, lacing them on the too-fat pillow, cupping her head. "Sheesh. I'm starting to feel as if I know you so well. But I don't even know where you live—in Bozeman, right?" He made a noise in the affirmative. "Your house...what's it like?"

"Four thousand square feet. Vaulted ceilings. Lots of windows. Good views."

"And redwood decking, on a number of levels— with a huge hot tub, right?"

"How did you know that?"

"Oh, Justin. How else could it be? And come on. Fair's fair. Women?"

He let out a big, fake sigh. "Okay. What do you need to know?"

She thought of the way he'd kissed her out in the shed—and when they got "married." And she realized it had never occurred to her that there might be someone special in his life. A live-in girlfriend, or even...

*A wife.*

No. No, that couldn't be. He could never have kissed her like that if there already was a special woman in his life—not the way he had when they'd pretended to get married.

And certainly not the way he'd kissed her out in the shed.

And if he *could*...

Oh, God. Here she'd made such a big deal about asking him if he was after her money. And she hadn't bothered to find out if he had a wife.

"It's too damn quiet over there." His voice was deep and rough—and teasing.

"Justin, are you married?"

There was dead silence, and then, "What the hell made you think that?"

"Nothing. It's just that I never asked—and you never said."

He swore under his breath. "I've done one or two things I'm not...thrilled I had to do, I'll admit." She wondered what, exactly. But before she had time to ask, he said, "But I never will do that—play one woman when I'm married to another." He sounded totally disgusted with the very idea.

Which pleased her greatly. "Er...that would be a no?"

"Yeah. A no. A *definite* no—and let me guess your next question. Do I have a steady woman in my life?"

She was grinning again. "Yep. That would be it."

"That's a no, too."

"Well." She put her arms down on the blankets again. "Okay, then. Were you *ever* married?"

"Never. Too busy making something from nothing. Serious relationships just didn't fit into the equation."

"You're career-driven?"

"I guess one of these days I'll have to slow down and get a life. But I like what I do."

"What about...a high school sweetheart?"

A brief silence, then, "High school. Now, that was a long time ago."

She realized she didn't know his age. "You're how old?"

"Thirty-two. And as I think I told you, when I was growing up, we moved around a lot—no chance to fit in. I dated now and then. It never went anywhere."

"You make yourself sound like a lonely guy."

He grunted. "No need for a pity party. There have been women, just not anything too deep or especially meaningful."

*There have been women…*

Well, of course there had. He had those compelling good looks. That kind of dangerous, mysterious air about him. A lot of women really went for the dangerous type. And yet, he could be so charming, so open, about himself and his life. And then there was the way he could kiss.…

Katie slipped her hand up, to touch her lips, remembering.

Oh, yes. A guy who could kiss like that would have had some practice.

But there was no special woman. No secret wife.

In spite of that aura of danger he could give off, Justin Caldwell was an honest guy—and Katie really did like that in a man.

The next day was Monday. They woke to find the snow still coming down, though not as thickly as the day before. On the ground, it reached halfway to the porch roof. After they'd dressed and had their fresh coffee and two-day-old sandwiches, they both went out to the front porch, though the door could barely clear the spill of snow that sloped onto the boards of the porch floor.

"Shoveling our way out of here will be a hell of a challenge," Justin said.

She nodded. "If it would only stop coming down. Give us a chance to take a crack at it, give the snowplow a break. It's piling up faster than anyone could hope to clear it."

Back inside, the phone was still out. And the boom box picked up the usual crackling static.

They made their way along the narrow covered path to the shed, where they spent a couple of hours cleaning up after Buttercup and keeping her company. Twice, the horse got feisty with Justin. She tried again to head-butt him into the hay. And once, in a deft move, she actually got the collar of his jacket between her teeth. She yanked it off him.

When he swore at her, she instantly dropped it. White tail swishing grandly, she turned for the doors that led out to a wall of snow.

"See?" he demanded. "That horse hates me."

"Could be affection," Katie suggested.

"Yeah, right." He picked up the old coat and brushed it off.

"Hey, at least it didn't land in a pile of manure."

He made a low sound, something halfway between a chuckle and a grunt, and slipped his arms into the sleeves. "Are we done here?"

She agreed that they were.

Back in the museum, Katie decided to get busy on the day's main project: clean hair.

Over her baggy tan pants, she put on a wrinkled white T-shirt with a boarded-up mine shaft and Stay Out, Stay Alive! emblazoned across the front. The rummage sale bags didn't come through with a bath towel. But hey. She had plenty of personal-size bottles of shampoo—in herbal scent and ''no tears.'' And there was a stack of dish towels in the kitchen cupboard. She'd make do with a few of them.

Then came the big internal debate—to use the bathroom sink: more private. Or the one in the kitchen: bigger.

Bigger won. Justin had seen her in her ugly sweater and saggy pants wearing zero makeup; he'd seen her in the distinctly unflattering flannel pajamas. He could certainly stand to get a look at her bending over a sink with her hair soaking wet.

Glamour just wasn't something a girl could maintain in a situation like this.

Justin sat at the table playing solitaire with a deck he'd found in the desk out front and tried not to sneak glances at Katie while she washed her hair.

The faint perfume from the shampoo filled the air, a moist, flowery scent. And the curve of her body as she bent over the sink, the shining coils of her wet hair, the creamy smoothness of her neck, bared with her hair tumbling into the sink, even the rushing sound of the water, the way it spilled over the vulnerable shape of her skull, turning her hair to a silken stream and dribbling over her satiny cheek and into her eyes....

He couldn't stop looking.

He had a problem. And he knew it.

There was something about her. Something soft and giving. Something tender and gentle and smart and funny…and sexy, too. All at the same time.

Something purely feminine.

Something that really got to him.

Every hour he spent with her, he wanted her more. It was starting to get damn tough—keeping it friendly. Not pushing too fast.

*Too fast?* He restrained a snort of heavy irony liberally laced with his own sexual frustration.

*Too fast* implied there would be satisfaction.

There wouldn't be. And he damn well had to keep that in mind.

Even if she said yes to him, there was no way he was taking her to bed while they were locked in here.

He couldn't afford that. Not without protection. And though the bags in the storage room seemed to have no end of useful items in them, what they didn't have were condoms.

He knew because he'd actually checked to see if they did.

And since he'd checked, he'd found himself thinking constantly of all the ways a man and a woman could enjoy each other sexually short of actual consummation.

He grabbed up a card to move it—and then couldn't resist stealing another look.

She'd rinsed away most of the flowery-scented shampoo, but there was a tiny froth of it left on her earlobe. She rinsed all around it, but somehow the water never quite reached it.

He gritted his teeth to keep from telling her to get that bit of lather on her ear. He ordered his body to stay in that chair. Every nerve seemed to sizzle.

Damned if he wasn't getting hard.

*Ridiculous,* he thought. *This has to stop....*

He looked down at the card in his hand—the jack of spades—and couldn't even remember what he'd meant to do with it.

This was bad. Real bad.

Some kind of dark justice?

Hell. Probably.

He meant to use her as another way to get to Caleb. Too bad he hadn't realized how powerfully—and swiftly—*she* would end up getting to *him.*

At last, she tipped her head enough that the water flowed over that spot on her ear. The little dab of lather rinsed away and down the drain.

Late that afternoon, Justin went out to the front of the museum to stoke the fire in the stove. Katie busied herself in the kitchen, putting away the few dishes that stood drying on the drain mat, wiping the table and the counters. The tasks were simple ones, easily accomplished.

After she rinsed the sponge and set it in the little tray by the sink, she found herself drawn to the window. She wandered over and stood there watching the snow falling through the graying light, wondering how long it would be until they could dig out, until the old mare in the shed got a little room to stretch her legs and a nice, big bucket of oats.

Justin returned from the front room. She glanced

over and gave him a smile and went back to gazing out at the white world beyond the glass.

He went to the sink. She heard the water running, was aware of his movements as he washed his hands and then reached for the towel. A moment later, she heard his approach, though she didn't turn to watch him come toward her.

It was so still out there. Snowy and silent. The museum sat at the corner, where Elk Avenue turned east. There was a full acre to either side, free of structures—what had, years ago, been part of the schoolyard. Katie could see the shadowy outline of the first house beyond the museum property. The Lockwoods lived there—a young couple with two children, a boy and a girl, eight and nine: Jeff and Kaylin, both nice kids. Kaylin loved to read. She and Jeff always attended the library's weekly children's story hour, run by Emelda Ross.

There was a light on in the Lockwood house, the gleam of it just visible, through the veil of falling snow. Katie hoped the Lockwoods were safe in there, with a cozy fire and plenty to eat.

"Katie…" Justin brushed a hand against her shoulder. The warm thrill his touch brought lightened her spirits—at least a little. "Watching it won't make it stop coming down."

She thought of the noisy beer drinkers back at the hall, of dear old Emelda, who'd stuck it out when all the other members of the Historical Society had left. "I was just thinking of everyone back at the hall. I hope they're all safe."

"They had food, didn't they?"

She looked from all that blinding white to the man beside her. "Yes. The potluck, remember? People brought all those casseroles."

"So they'll get by." He gave her a steady look, a look meant to reassure. "They have food. And restrooms. Water—and the sidewalks on Main are all covered. That's going to make it a lot easier for them to get out than it will be for us."

He was right. She added, "And the first place the snowplow will be working is up and down Main."

"See? They'll be okay."

But there were others—the ones who'd left the hall before Katie and Justin. "What about the people who left for home? We don't even know if they all made it."

He took her by the shoulders—firmly, but gently. His touch caused the usual reactions: butterflies in her stomach, a certain warmth lower down....

"Katie, you can't do anything about it. We just have to make the best of a tough situation. And so will everyone else."

In her mind's eye, she saw Addy's dear long, aristocratic face, her sparkling blue eyes and her prim little smile—and then she pictured Caleb, in that white Stetson he liked to wear, a corner of his mouth quirked up in his rascal's grin. "I don't even know where Addy and Caleb went. One minute they were there, in the hall, and then, when we were up there on the stage, just before the 'Reverend' Green stepped up, I looked out over the crowd and I didn't see either of them."

"They probably went home. Or maybe you just

didn't spot them and they're both still there. Either way, there's not a damn thing you can do about it. Just let yourself believe they're safe—which, most likely, they are.''

"But if—''

He didn't let her finish. ''Worrying about them won't help them. All it'll do is make *you* miserable.''

"But I only—''

"It'll be okay.'' He shook her, lightly. ''Got it?''

She made herself give him a nod.

He studied her for a long moment. Then he demanded, ''Why the hell do you still look so worried, then?''

She only shrugged. What was there to say? He was right. There was no point in worrying. But when she thought of Addy and Caleb—when she looked at the Lockwood's faint light across the snow-covered museum yard—she simply couldn't help it.

"Hey,'' Justin murmured. ''Hey, come on…'' He pulled her to him.

She didn't even consider resisting—why should she? Maybe she'd had her doubts about him at first. But gently and tenderly, he'd dispelled her reservations. She knew she could trust him now.

He wrapped those long, hard arms around her and she pressed herself close to him, tucking her head under his chin, laying her ear against the leaping reindeers on the front of his sweater, right over his heart, which beat steady and strong, if a little too fast. She smiled to herself—a woman's smile. His embrace brought more comfort than words could. And the sound of his heartbeat, racing in time to hers?

That wasn't comforting, not in the least. That sound thrilled her. It stole her breath.

She hoped—she *prayed*—that everyone else trapped by the storm was at least safe and warm with plenty to eat.

For herself, though, there was no place she would rather be than right here in the Thunder Canyon Historical Museum held close and safe in Justin's arms.

For herself, she was beginning to believe that getting snowed-in with Caleb's business associate was the best thing that had ever happened to her.

She felt his lips against her hair and snuggled closer. "Justin?"

"Hmm?"

She tipped her head up to find those blue eyes waiting.

And his lips…

It just seemed the most natural thing. To lift her mouth, to let her eyes drift shut.

His mouth touched hers—so lightly. Heat flared and flowed through her. Her lips burned. Her pulse raced.

Then he lifted away.

She didn't want that.

Oh, no. She wanted more. Much more.

"Justin?" She opened her eyes to look up at him again.

"Hmm?"

"Justin, do you like kissing me?"

He muttered something very low, probably a swear word. "I do. I like it too damn much."

"I like kissing you, too," she confessed. "I like it a lot."

His gaze scanned her face. "So…?"

She slid her hands up to encircle his neck. "Please. Kiss me some more."

"Katie," he whispered, and that was all. Then his mouth swooped down and covered hers.

## Chapter Six

They kissed, standing there at the window, with the white hush of the snow drifting down outside, for the longest, sweetest time. When Justin finally lifted his head, he asked, husky and low, "Convinced?"

She blinked up at him. "Of what?"

"That I like kissing you?"

She pretended to consider that question—which, truthfully, required no consideration at all—and then at last, she said, "I think you should kiss me again— just to make sure."

"Ah. To make sure…"

"That's right."

He cupped her face—cradled it, really. His hands were warm and cherishing against her cheeks. And then he lowered his head again and his mouth touched hers and…

Oh, there was nothing like it. Kissing Justin.

Kissing Justin was everything kissing ought to be. His mouth played on hers and his arms slid around her to hold her close and she felt his heart beating, hard and steady, against her breasts, keeping pace with hers.

That time, when he lifted his head, she said in a voice gone husky with pleasure, "I'm getting it now. You like kissing me."

"Yeah. I do."

And to prove it, he kissed her again—a hard, deep, long one that melted her midsection and turned her knees to rubber.

She clutched his shoulders and sagged against him, feeling very aroused, totally shameless. She liked this feeling. She liked it a lot. There was so much she'd been missing. Not anymore, though. "I don't know. If you're going to *keep* kissing me, I might just have to sit down."

"Let me help you with that." He grabbed the nearest chair, spun it around and dropped into it—pulling her with him, onto his lap.

Her breath hitched as she landed.

"Better?" he asked.

"Oh, I think…"

He nuzzled her neck, pressed a burning kiss at the place where her pulse beat close to the skin. A lovely shiver went through her and she sighed.

"You think what?" He breathed the words against her throat—and then he caught her earlobe between his teeth. He worried it, lightly, as she clutched his shoulders and sighed some more.

"Oh, Justin…"

His tongue touched the place where his teeth had been, a velvety moist caress. He licked the tender hollow behind her earlobe. Briefly, with the very tip of that bold tongue, he dipped into her ear.

She let out a low moan. She was supposed to be telling him…something. The question was what. "I…well…"

He threaded his fingers up into her hair and he brushed a line of butterfly-light kisses along her jaw. "What you think…"

"Think?" The word sounded alien. Not surprising. At that moment, thinking was the last thing on her mind.

He cradled the back of her head, holding her still, bringing his mouth a breath's distance from hers. "You were telling me…what you think…"

"I…well…"

One corner of his mouth lifted in a knowing smile. "Well, what?"

"I forgot." And she had.

She'd forgotten everything. Nothing mattered, at that moment, but this man and the drugging pleasure of his hands on her body, his mouth so close to hers. "Kiss me. Again."

He obeyed. His mouth covered hers and she wrapped her arms around his neck and kissed him back with boundless enthusiasm.

This time when they came up for air, he took her by the waist and held her away from him. "We'd better stop." His voice was rough—almost curt.

She started to argue. She didn't want to stop. But

maybe he was right. Where could they go from here, except to the bed with the pineapple finials?

Was she ready for that yet?

As much as she liked kissing him and feeling his hands on her body…as much as she liked *him*…as much as she couldn't help but start to think that there was something very special going on here, between them…

That was a big, fat…maybe. Even given what she'd decided that morning—about the lack of sex of any kind in her life, about how she was going to stop being a cliché. Even given all that, well, they didn't need to rush this, did they? There was nothing that said they couldn't take their time. Though she was determined to get herself a sex life one of these days very soon—and with Justin—she *was* old-fashioned in some ways. She believed making love should be special. And it *shouldn't* be rushed.

He smoothed a wild curl of hair off her cheek. "Listen." His eyes teased—and burned, too. "I want you to get up. And I want you to do it very carefully."

She frowned, and then she understood. Oh, my. Yes. She could *feel* him and it was just like out in the shed the day before. He was very happy to be near her.

"Oh. Oh, well. You're, uh—"

"Katie."

"Uh. Yeah?"

"We don't need a lot of discussion here."

"Oh. Well, no. Of course, we don't." She put her feet on the floor and stood, backing off a little. Her gaze dropped to—oops. Blinking, she yanked her chin up and gave him a nervous smile. "Is that better?"

"Not really." The chair legs scraped the floor as he turned to face the table—a deft movement, in spite of the pained grunt that accompanied it. Now his lap, and the obvious bulge there, was hidden by the tabletop. "In a few minutes, I'll be fine."

"Well. Good."

He folded his hands on the tabletop. "It would help if you wouldn't stand there looking so damn... thoroughly kissed."

Her wobbly smile widened. "But Justin. I *am* thoroughly kissed."

He commanded sternly, "Think of an activity. One that doesn't involve kissing."

She pretended to give his request great thought. "Well, now...we could go out and visit Buttercup again."

He scowled. "Let me qualify. Something that doesn't involve kissing *or* that mean old mare."

"Hmm. It's a tough one."

He shifted in his chair, wincing. "Work with it."

An idea came to her. "I know. We could tour the museum."

"Why? I've seen it."

"Now, wait a minute. I'll admit, you've seen about all there is to see in the central room. But the two side rooms...why, Justin, you've hardly had a look. And you know, on second thought, you've only *slept* in the central room. That's not the same as a tour."

He let out a dry chuckle. "I've been up close and

personal with that dinky narrow cot of mine. Isn't that enough?''

"Oh, no. You have to see it all. I insist. The rich and varied history of Thunder Canyon is right here, only a few steps away. You owe it to yourself to explore it.''

"I can't wait.''

"Don't get so excited,'' she instructed, deadpan.

He tipped his head toward his lap. "I'm trying.''

She couldn't help it, she burst into a laugh—and then she frowned. "You know, now I think about it, it's not really fair that I always get the big bed.''

"Katie. I'm fine with the cot.''

"But still, it's only right that we—''

"Stop. I *love* that cot of mine and you can't have it. Now, I want you to go on ahead of me, reconnoiter the display rooms, get your tour guide rap down pat. Let me, er, relax a little here.''

She decided not to remark on what might need relaxing. "Hey, we could even take some rags in there, dust the display cases…''

He sent her a pained look. "The fun never ends.''

She was dusting a case full of old gold-panning equipment in the south room when he joined her. She handed him a rag and one of the two bottles of spray cleaner she'd found in the storage room.

"I thought this was a tour,'' he groused. But he was grinning as he took the rag and bottle.

"The museum is a community effort,'' she told him tartly. "We all have to pitch in.''

"Hey. I'm all for that." He saluted her with the spray bottle.

They set to work dusting the cases. As they sprayed and polished, she explained about the Montana gold rush that had begun in Idaho, with the Salmon River strike. "Gold fever came to Montana in 1862. John White and company, en route to the Salmon River mines, found gold on the way—at Grasshopper Creek." She paused to point out the exact location on the big laminated territorial map on the wall. "Bannack—" She pointed again. "—Montana's first boomtown, sprang up during that rush."

"Just like in the reenactment Saturday."

"That's right." She beamed at him. "For a man who didn't have the benefit of a Montana education, you're a very good student."

"Thank you. I try."

"Shall I continue?"

"By all means."

So she explained that the gold rush had lasted into the early 1890s, starting with placer mining and then, as the streams petered out, panning and sluicing gave way to hardrock mining. "There were a number of mines right here in the Thunder Canyon area. Caleb still owns one, as a matter of fact. It's called the Queen of Hearts."

"So I heard."

"From Caleb?"

"More or less." At her questioning look, he explained, "I'm in business with Caleb. My people have gone over his books, with Caleb's full knowledge and consent, of course. As a result, I know a lot about what his assets are, as well as which pies he's got his fingers in. I understand the gold mine's been shut down for years. 'Played out,' isn't that what they say in the trade?''

"That's exactly what they say—and I'll bet you didn't know that Caleb's great-grandfather, Amos Douglas, won the Queen in a card game." She sprayed and rubbed with her cloth. "Or so the legend goes."

"Fascinating."

She glanced his way, and found he was watching her. Her body went warm all over. "Less staring, more cleaning," she advised.

Once they'd finished in the mining display, she took him to the central room, where they dusted the tables and she told him the origins of the most interesting pieces.

She gestured grandly with her dusting rag in the direction of the big bed with the pineapple finials and the heavy, dark bureaus, vanity set, bed tables and chairs that surrounded it. "This bedroom suite was used at the Lazy D during Amos Douglas's time. It's of the finest mahogany."

"Only the best for the Douglases." There was something in his tone—something way too ironic, even cynical. She sent him a puzzled look, but he only shrugged and bent to dust a bedside table.

And she had to agree with him. "It's true. Only the best. For generations, the Douglases have been the wealthiest, most influential family in the area."

"Don't forget to dust those pineapples."

"That's right. If you don't watch it, I may still have

to throw one at you. I want it dust-free if I do.'' She reached up—but the intricately carved end-piece was too high. She couldn't get her rag around it.

Justin stepped closer. ''Allow me.''

Her pulse kicked up a notch, just to have him standing so near, eyes gleaming at her with humor and heat. ''Oh, by all means.'' She bowed and moved back and he did the honors.

Once every surface in the central room had been wiped clean of dust, they proceeded to the north addition, where the personal artifacts of life in Territorial and early-statehood Montana waited to be admired—and the cases that protected them, dusted.

Justin went straight to the tall case containing a mannequin in a faded red satin dress. Cinched tight at the wasp-thin waste, the dress had a deep neckline and lots of black lace trim. The mannequin wore several ropes of fake pearls around her neck, a thick bracelet of glittering jet stones and an ostrich feather in her pinned-up hair. In one hand, she carried a black fan edged with lace. The other hand held the red skirt high, revealing a froth of red and black petticoats—and a fancy black silk garter.

Justin wolf-whistled. ''Love that red dress.''

Katie grinned. ''That dress belonged to one of Thunder Canyon's most memorable early citizens. The Shady Lady, Lily Divine.''

''Is this the part where I say, 'Ooh-la-la'?''

''That would be appropriate, yes. Back in, oh, 1890 or so, Lily owned the Shady Lady Sporting House and Saloon. The building still stands at the corner of Main and Thunder Canyon Road, though the place is now a restaurant and bar called the Hitching Post. The original bar from the Shady Lady is still there, in the building. And a very risqué painting of Lily hangs above it.''

"Risqué, how?"

"In it she wears nothing but a few wisps of strategically draped semitransparent cloth.''

"I have to see that.''

"And if it ever stops snowing, you just might.''

He tipped his head toward the low case beside the mannequin in the red dress. "A few of Lily Divine's things, I take it?''

"That's right.'' Katie moved in beside him. They looked down at the tortoise shell dresser set in a gold floral design studded with rhinestones, at the black lace gloves and the faded filmy undergarments. There was even a corset—a black one, dripping with red silk ribbons.

"It looks to me like the Shady Lady was a very fun gal.''

Katie shrugged. "So they say. And not only fun, but a suffragist, as well. Or so some accounts claim.'' He looked up from the case and when their eyes met, she realized she never wanted to look away.

*Back to the Shady Lady,* some wiser voice in the distant recesses of her mind instructed.

She tuned out that wiser voice. "Oh, Justin…'' The two words escaped her lips, full of hope and longing, and having nothing at all to do with either the notorious Lily Divine, or with getting the dusting done.

He whispered her name.

Her heart seemed to expand in the prison of her chest.

And at that moment, *not* to kiss him…

Well, that was impossible. It just wouldn't do.

She set down her rag and her spray bottle on the glass case beside her. He did the same.

"Justin," she whispered, thinking she should really try a little harder to resist the overwhelming urge to feel his lips on hers.

"Katie…"

A long moment elapsed. She looked at him and he looked back at her and—

"Oh, Justin, I think we're in trouble here."

He only nodded. His eyes said he knew exactly what kind of trouble she meant.

"We shouldn't," she whispered. "We told ourselves we wouldn't."

"That's right," he agreed, his voice rough and low. "No more kissing."

"It's not a good idea."

"Things could…get out of control."

"Easily."

"It's crazy."

"Wild…"

"Dangerous…"

"Oh, I know," she said.

And then he reached for her.

With a glad cry, she reached back. His arms went around her and all doubt fled.

Eager and oh-so-willing, she lifted her mouth to receive his kiss.

## Chapter Seven

"We...have to...be careful..." He whispered the words between quick, hungry kisses.

She nodded. "Oh. Yes. Careful. You're so right."

His mouth closed on hers again, drugging. Magical. She slid her hands up his broad chest to wrap them around his neck, and he caught her wrists. He guided them down, so her arms were straight at her sides.

His fingers slipped over the backs of her hands and he wove them between hers, lightly rubbing—in and out and in again, never quite clasping, flesh brushing flesh, little tingles of excitement zipping through her with every featherlight caress. All the while, as his fingers teased hers, he kissed her, his tongue sweeping her mouth, his lips hot and soft and oh-so-tender.

She moaned as he finally twined his fingers with hers, tightening, curling his hands to fists, so her hands were cradled in his palms, her fingers captured between his. A thoroughly willing captive, she smiled against his lips as he guided her hands around behind her.

Their joined fists resting at the small of her back, he kissed her some more. She sighed at the wonder of it, and gave her mouth up to his.

After forever of the two of them kissing and kissing as if they would never stop, he began walking her backward.

She stumbled at first, surprised. A giddy laugh escaped her; he chuckled in response.

Quickly, she regained her balance, and, as he guided her, she backed up toward the open door to the central room. It was like a dance, a beautiful, slow, erotic dance.

He waltzed her through the open doorway, his mouth locked to hers. On they went, slow, delicious step by slow step, to the turn in the roped-off walkway, and then down toward the wide, high bed that had once graced a guest room at the Lazy D.

There, with only a stretch of rope keeping them from the waiting bed, he paused. She swayed in his hold, her mouth fused to his.

A small cry of loss escaped her when he lifted his head. He eased his strong fingers free of hers and stepped back.

"We should stop now."

For a suspended moment, she gazed up into his gleaming eyes. And then, with a sigh, she rested her head on his shoulder. "You know, you keep saying that."

His arms closed around her, tight and warm. She felt the sweet brush of his lips in her hair as she breathed in the scent of him: of the motel-issue shampoo they'd both used, of his clean skin and a faint hint of the inexpensive aftershave he'd found in the brown bag. "I know I keep saying it," he muttered against her hair. "I just don't seem to be *listening* to myself when I say it."

She lifted her head and captured his blue, blue gaze again. Boldly, she suggested, "We could just go ahead and slip under the rope. We could kick off our shoes, stretch out on the bed...."

His arms dropped away. "And then what?"

She swallowed. "Well, and then, we could...take it from there."

"Take it from there," he repeated, gruffly. "I'd like that. Way too much. But we can't lose our heads here. We've got to be sensible."

Now she was the one repeating after *him*. "Sensible."

"That's what I said."

"I have to admit, I don't feel all that sensible recently. Not since I met you."

That brought a smile to his beautiful mouth. "All my fault, then."

She tipped her chin higher. "No. This thing between us, it's fifty-fifty. You're not leading me anywhere I don't want to go."

He studied her face for a long moment—long enough that she felt a blush begin to burn her cheeks. And then he said flatly, "I've got no condoms. I don't suppose you do?"

"Uh. No. Sorry." She looked down, not embarrassed, exactly, but definitely feeling in over her head.

He put a finger under her chin and made her look at him again. "It's something that has to be considered."

"Oh, I know. You're right. I just…well, we could be careful, couldn't we?"

He swore under his breath. "I keep telling myself the same thing. But I don't feel all that damn careful, and that's the hard truth. Once I get my arms around you, caution flies right out the door."

"I could…be cautious for us." Even as she suggested it, she knew that wouldn't work. When he kissed her, words like *careful* and *caution* vanished from her vocabulary.

He gave her a rueful smile. "No doubt about it. Time to go out and check on that mean mare."

The snow stopped around seven. They were sitting at the table eating applesauce and more of the never-ending sandwiches, when Katie looked across at the light in the Lockwood's window and realized there was no curtain of white obscuring it.

Justin noticed, too. "Tomorrow we can probably start digging out."

"Hey, the phone may even be working soon." She'd checked it just a half an hour before. "And if the snow doesn't start in heavy again, the plow should get to us by tomorrow sometime."

"And we'll be free."

They stared at each other across the expanse of the

tabletop. "Free…" She repeated the word softly. And somehow, she couldn't keep from sounding forlorn.

She looked out the window again, at that golden light from the house across the museum yard.

No question that stale sandwiches, wearing other people's ill-fitting cast-off clothes, and sponge baths at the sink in the ladies' room got old very fast. She'd be grateful for a shower, something different to eat, her own clothes to wear. And more than any of those minor inconveniences, it would be a huge relief to know that everyone she cared about had come through the unexpected blizzard safe and sound.

But still. They *had* made themselves a private little world here, in the center of the storm. She would miss it—miss just the two of them, all alone. Talking through the night. Kissing. Laughing together. And kissing some more.…

She would miss it a lot.

Would she see Justin again, once they were out of here?

She frowned. Well, of course she would. Really, she didn't need to even ask herself the question.

They had a…connection, something special going on between them. She felt it in her bones. This was different from anything she'd known before. Even after what had happened with Ted Anders and Jackson Tully, she had no doubts about Justin.

None at all.

He spoke then. "For someone who's probably going to be out of this place tomorrow, you're looking pretty glum."

She turned from the golden light across the way to

meet his waiting eyes. "I want to see you again, when this is over. Do you want to see me?" She was proud, of the steadiness of her voice, that she'd put her own intention right out there, hadn't waited for him to make the first move, handing him all the power and then hoping he'd give her a call.

Oh, yes. Katie Fenton, a cliché no more.

"I do want to see you again. I want that very much."

Her heart leaped—and then something in his eyes spoke to her. Something…not right. "But?"

He blinked. "No buts. I want to see you when we get out of here."

*And I will.* She thought the words he didn't say.

The silence stretched out. Painful. Empty. She wanted to demand, *And will you?* But somehow, that seemed one step too far. He should say it of his own accord, or not at all.

She wanted him. She *cared* for him. She had no doubt that he wanted and cared for her.

Would it go any further than that?

That secret something behind his eyes was telling her no. "Justin?"

"Yeah?"

"Is there…something else you want to say to me?"

Justin looked at the incredible woman across from him and never wanted to look away.

His chest felt tight—as if something strong and relentless was squeezing it. His gut twisted.

The urge was there, in his clenched gut and his tight chest—an urge almost too powerful to deny.

To tell her everything. To throw over his carefully constructed plans.

To lay it all out for her: what Caleb really was to him and how he meant to make the older man pay for the cruel things he'd done.

To hit her with the whole truth: how from the first night fate threw them together, he'd felt the heat between them and decided to make use of it, to toss her into the mix. How he'd purposely set out to take advantage of the situation, and of her.

It was crazy, even to think he might open his mouth and…

No.

He wasn't going to blow it. He'd waited too long to get to the man who'd ruined his mother's hope and happiness. He had to remember….

All of it. The times she didn't come home until he was sick with fear and worry. The nights she *was* home, when he'd wake and have that strange, lost feeling and come out of his room to find her at the kitchen table or curled up on the couch, her eyes swollen and red from crying, the end of her cigarette glowing like a burning eye in the dark.

He had to remember….

The suicide attempts. The never-ending new starts that always went wrong. Caleb's name on her lips like an unanswered prayer the day that she died….

Of lung cancer. She never would give up those damn cigarettes until the last few months of her life. And by then it was too late. Lung cancer got her—

but Caleb Douglas killed her as sure as if he'd put a gun to her head and pulled the trigger.

Caleb Douglas broke her heart and she never did find a way to mend it again. Justin, just a kid, had been powerless to help her.

He wasn't powerless anymore.

And damned if he was giving up now.

He was set on a course and it was a just course. What he would do was perfectly legal; he had the power now—power Caleb himself had put in his hands—and he would use it.

In the end, if all went according to plan, there would be big profits for everyone. Including Caleb.

That was the beauty of it. Everybody would win.

At least in terms of the bottom line.

He only wished…

*Wished.*

It was a word for fools, for helpless little boys who spent too much time alone, for boys with no fathers, whose mothers too seldom came home.…

He wasn't a little boy anymore.

And he wasn't going to spew his guts to anyone— not even to sweet Katie Fenton who was turning out to be a hell of a lot more woman than he'd ever bargained for.

Those amber eyes were still waiting.

He couldn't stand the disappointment he saw in them. "I *want* to see you when we get out of here, Katie. I want to see you and I *will.*"

*And I will.*

Now, where the hell had that come from?

He'd been so careful. He'd never actually lied to her.

Not until now.

But then again, he *did* want to see her again.

Though he knew damn well he shouldn't, he wanted to keep on seeing her. He wanted...

A whole hell of a lot more with her than he was ever going to get.

He shouldn't have lied. But the words were out now. No calling them back. In future, he'd just have to keep a closer watch on his tongue.

He silently vowed he would do just that as she watched him with worried eyes.

## Chapter Eight

Katie opened her eyes to the sight of the shadowed rafters overhead.

For a second or two, with the soft mist of sleep still fogging her mind, she wondered where she was.

And then she placed herself: the four-poster bed in the Historical Museum. With no windows to let in the light from outside, she couldn't begin to guess what time it was. There *was* one clock. An intricate gold leaf ormolu piece with Cupid strumming a lyre perched on top. It sat on the mantel in the "parlor" area.

She couldn't see the face of it from the bed. Plus, it wasn't wound and always read ten-fifteen.

And what did it matter, anyway, what time it was? She and Justin weren't going anywhere until the snowplow finally showed up. They could sleep all day and stay up all night. There was no schedule, just whatever suited them.

*Justin…*

What was going on with him?

There had been a certain…reserve—a new distance between them, since dinnertime, when she told him she wanted to see him after they got out of here and asked him if *he* wanted to see her.

He'd definitely withdrawn from her after that. From then on, when she spoke, he gave her single-sentence replies. When she looked at him, his gaze would slide away. Also, it had seemed to her that he was careful to avoid touching her. He kept his distance emotionally—and physically, too.

All evening she'd told herself to let it be. The guy didn't have to be hanging on her every word every minute of the day. Maybe he just wanted a little time to himself. In such close quarters, there was no easy way for him to claim some private space.

But in her heart, she knew it wasn't about lack of privacy. It was about them seeing each other after they got out of here.

It hurt a lot, to admit it to herself, but she was beginning to think she'd gotten things all wrong. She'd read more into this thing between them than was actually there.

Oh, not in terms of herself. She knew how she felt. It was real and strong and…maybe it was love.

Or something very close to it—something that *could* be love, given the time and space to grow.

But just because she was feeling something didn't automatically mean he had to feel it in return.

She'd gone to bed, however long ago that had been, ahead of him. And she'd lain here waiting for him.

He'd yet to come in when she finally fell asleep.

Was he even here now?

She sat up.

Across the room, the too-short, too-narrow cot lay empty, the star quilt smooth and undisturbed, the flat little pillow without a wrinkle.

He hadn't even come to bed.

Quietly, carefully—as if there was someone in the empty room she might disturb should she make a sound—she lay back down.

And popped right back up again.

No. This was wrong. If he didn't want to get anything going with her, well, that was his prerogative and she would learn to accept it.

But she wasn't going to just lie here, worrying. And what about tomorrow? What about whatever time they had left here until the plow came? If she spent that time tiptoeing around him, keeping her head down and her mouth shut, well, wouldn't that be just like the woman she'd told herself she wasn't going to be anymore? Wouldn't that be like Katie, the cliché?

She needed to clear the air between them.

How, exactly, to do that, she wasn't quite sure. But it certainly wouldn't get done with her lying here in bed agonizing over what had gone wrong and him off somewhere in another room doing whatever the heck he was doing.

She shoved the covers back and slid her stocking feet to the floor.

\* \* \*

"Justin."

He turned from his own dark reflection in the window to find Katie standing in the doorway to the central room, wearing her wrinkled red pajamas and a pair of fat wool socks, blinking against the bright overhead kitchen light.

A slow warmth spread through him, just to see her standing there. It was that feeling of well-being and contented relief a man gets when he comes in from the cold and finds a cheery fire waiting—that feeling multiplied about a thousand times.

Damn, she looked good, all squinty-eyed with a sleep mark on her soft cheek and her dark hair a tangled halo all around her sweet face. Had there ever been a woman so outright adorable? Not in his experience, and that had been varied, if not especially meaningful.

She stuck out a hand in the direction of the book that lay open on the table in front of him. "Still on chapter three, I'll bet."

He glanced down at the book in question, then back up at her, an ironic smile twisting his lips. "Page sixty-seven, to be exact."

She wrapped her arms around herself. Her soft mouth was pursed tight. "Look. Mind if I sit down?"

The set of her mouth, the determined look in her eyes, her defensive posture—they all told him more than he wanted to know.

No doubt about it. Katie had questions.

Which meant he would have to try to answer them honestly, but without ever telling her the whole truth.

Things got ugly when a man had too much to hide. He probably should have known that when he started this whole charade. Hell. He *had* known it. And he'd been willing to live with the ugliness.

Then.

He gave her an elaborately casual shrug and closed the book. "Sure. Take a seat."

She marched over, yanked out the chair opposite him, and plunked herself down into it, unwrapping her arms from around herself and folding her hands in her lap.

"Okay…" He drew the word out, eyeing her sideways. "What's up?"

She craned around to get a look at the kitchen clock. When she faced him again, she replied, "Well, *you* are. It's three-fifteen in the morning and you're just sitting here, staring out the window."

He lounged back in his chair, displaying an ease he didn't feel. "And this is a problem for you?"

"No. No, of course not." She huffed out a frustrated-sounding breath. "You can sit here all night if you want. What's bothering me is…" She ran out of steam, sucked in another big breath, and started again. "Look. I spent most of last night staying out of your way, and *you* spent most of it avoiding looking, talking or getting too close to me. I just, well, I'd like that to stop and I came out here to ask you what I could do to make that happen."

Her distress was palpable. He hated to see her so miserable, and he hated worst of all that he was the cause of her unhappiness.

But what the hell did he have to tell her?

Half-truths.

And when half-truths failed him, outright lies.

He wanted out of this—out of this damned museum, away from the reality that he was using her.

He didn't want to use her anymore. It had been a bad idea from the first and he wanted to walk away from it.

But there was no walking away now. The damage was done. She cared for him. When it all went down, she would be hurt, and hurt bad. There was no getting away from that now.

Even if he gave up his original plan to see that Caleb Douglas paid—which he wasn't about to do—he would still end up hurting her. It was simply too late to walk away and leave her untouched.

*Untouched.*

An interesting word choice given the plain fact that all he wanted to do was reach out.

And touch…

"Justin," she prompted, when he went too long without answering her. "Did you hear one thing I said to you?" A deep frown creased her brow.

He resisted the powerful urge to rise, to go to her, to smooth that frown away. "I heard you. Every word. Go on."

"Ahem. Well. The truth is I know very well why I stayed out of your way—because it seemed to me that you were avoiding me. *Were* you?"

"Yeah." What else was there to say? "I was."

"Why?"

*Why?* He should have known that one was coming. What to say now? How to weasel out of this one…

And then, out of nowhere, the exact right words seemed to well up of their own accord. "Because I want you. Because I want to *be* with you. And because it scares the hell out of me, that I do—and how much I do."

The words took form and he let them out and...

Damned if they weren't the absolute truth. More truth than he wanted to face himself, let alone share with her.

But he *had* shared them.

What did that mean?

Where was he headed with this?

Hell if he even knew.

Her soft face had gone softer still, all the worried tension melting out of it. Her eyes shone and her pursed-up mouth had relaxed to its usual sweet fullness. "Oh, Justin..." She lifted a hand from her lap and stretched it across the table to him. "Come on. Take a chance. Take a chance on me."

And before he could think twice, he was leaning toward her, reaching right back. Their hands met and heat shot up his arm, broke into a million swift, burning arrows that splintered off in all directions, hitting every nerve in his body at once.

All he could say was one word: her name. "Katie."

And then, as one, they stood. They stepped around the barrier of the table and there was a moment—painful and electric—when he almost managed to make himself let go, almost stepped back, almost told her, *Katie, I can't. Can't touch you, can't hold you...*

But the pull was too strong. It wouldn't be denied.

He gathered her in and she landed against him, soft

and warm and so willing, smelling of shampoo and sweetness, naked beneath the fuzzy red flannel.

"Katie." He buried his face in her fragrant hair. "Katie."

She nuzzled his chest, pressed her lips there, sent a warm, thrilling breath through the wool of the old sweater. The warmth spread, borne on that breath, a caress of hope and life itself. He held her tighter.

And she turned her head, pressing her mouth to his neck, a velvety pressure. Her lips opened slightly. He felt the wet brush of her tongue.

He groaned deep in his throat and an answering sound came from her, a soft, heated, purring sound. It vibrated through him, that sound, right down to the core of him.

He felt himself harden in an instant, and he did what he had to do, what he longed to do, sliding his hands down, over the tempting swell of her hips and under, tucking her into him, making her feel him, feel his need and his hunger.

She gasped, the sound purely female, speaking better than any words could of her eagerness, of her complete surrender.

*Mine.* The word exploded in his brain, bright as a shooting star in a dark winter world. *Mine.*

She gasped again and she tipped her head back, offering her mouth.

He took it, his blood roaring in his ears, his body burning, on fire.

All his lies, all his scheming, his lifelong quest for justice—all that was nothing. There was only Katie, the promise of Katie, the *truth* of Katie, held close in his hungry arms.

As he plunged his tongue into her eager mouth and cupped her bottom in his hands, pressing her harder into him, as his blood pounded through his veins and his heart beat so hard it was like thunder in his ears, he knew....

This...*this* was what mattered. This woman's tender heart, her lips, her breath, her yearning, willing body.

This was his truth. His real justice.

The truth that could save him.

The truth he could never claim.

He knew he had to stop this, that he owed it to her.

Somehow, from some deep hidden resource of rightness within him, he managed to break the never-ending kiss.

He tore his mouth from hers, groaning at the effort. "Katie."

But she only reached up, touched his mouth and whispered, "Shh, it's okay."

He bit the soft pad of her finger. She cried out— not in pain; it had been a gentle bite—but in hunger, with a fire that answered his own.

Her cry of need broke him. His last resistance shattered into a thousand tiny shards. He surrendered to the pounding of his own blood, the yearning like fire spreading through his veins.

She pulled her hand from his mouth and he cupped her head and claimed her lips again.

He kissed her and she kissed him back and he took a step and she moved with him.

No stumbling, not this time. Backward she went, knowing where he guided her, through the open door to the central room, down the roped-off walkway to...

The big, old bed with the pineapple finials, the bed that had once stood in a Douglas bedroom over a hundred years ago.

Was that irony?

Probably.

Did it matter? Did he care?

Not right then. Right then, there was nothing and no one but Katie in the world.

Nothing mattered, nothing even existed, but her tender lips and the wetness beyond, her soft, willing body, her eager sighs, the light and heat that seemed to radiate from her, warming him down to a place that, until she had found him, had lain forever cold, forever shadowed.

A place unknown even to him.

He held her close, his willing prisoner, with one arm. With the other he reached back, found the hook that held the thick rope to the pole and released it.

He let it drop. With a heavy, final thumping sound, it hit the hardwood floor.

She clasped his shoulders.

And then *she* was the one waltzing *him* backward, around the carved trunk at the end of the bed, to the knotted rag rug that waited beside it.

She pushed him onto the tangled blankets. The bed was high; he had to lift himself up to it, and he did, with little effort, bringing her with him, so she rested on top of him, a tempting pressure all along the length of him.

Until he rolled and captured her beneath him.

"Oh!" Her lids fluttered open and he looked for the briefest, sweetest moment into those honey-brown eyes. "Oh…" And her lashes settled, feather-soft, against her cheeks.

He shut his own eyes and lost himself in the sensation.

Of kissing her. Of touching her.

He slid to the side a little and put his weight on one arm, bringing the other up, laying his hand between her small, soft breasts, feeling the heat of her and beneath that, the strong, hungry beating of her heart.

The buttonholes on the old pajamas were worn and loose. The red plastic buttons slipped free with no difficulty at all. He undid them, one by one, only pausing when he once again got so lost in her kiss he could do nothing but press his mouth tighter to hers.

When all the buttons were undone, he eased the sides of the top open to reveal her beautiful white breasts. He took one in his hand.

"Oh," she cried, and "Oh!" again, as he positioned the hard, pink little nipple for his mouth.

He took it, closing his lips around it, and she moaned as he caught it lightly in his teeth and flicked his tongue across it, felt the puckered nub of flesh tighten all the more. She arched her back and clutched his head, her fingers threaded in his hair. He drew on her sweetness and more cries escaped her. The pleading, hungry sounds enflamed him, driving him on.

To know her.

In spite of everything, in spite of the lies he'd told

and the harm he would do her. To know her, anyway, in the deepest, most complete way.

To find the truth in spite of himself, here, in this moment, in the dark windowless quiet, with the artifacts of other, long-lost lives all around them.

Here among the ghosts of the past.

His body on fire with her, her scent all around him, her yielding flesh under his hands, his heart pounding out her name, it seemed to him he could sense them, those long-lost souls, that he could *feel* them.

The pioneers who came before. The hopeful families seeking a brighter future, the miners struck hard by gold fever, scouring streams, digging into mountainsides, after a fortune destined to elude all but a fortunate few. The merchants, the cattle barons, the Shady Lady in her red dress, lounging provocatively against the bar in her sporting house saloon.

They came to Thunder Canyon with desperate ambition, a grasping, undaunted will to match his own. How many found the dreams they sought?

It was too long ago. He would never know.

He only knew that, for this night, in this moment, he held the happiness he'd never understood he was seeking. *She* was his happiness.

He couldn't hold her past this night. Cold, hard reality *would* intrude. He knew that, too.

But for now, for this brief time in this old bed with Katie in his arms, he was someone else.

He was…

Her groom. And she was his sweet mail-order bride, come in on the train intending to marry a stranger—himself—and start a new life with him out here in the raw, untamed West.

They had said their vows before a drunken crowd of well-wishers and the buckboard pulled by the mean old palomino mare had brought them here.

A sudden blizzard had snowed them in, forcing them, with astonishing swiftness, to know each other.

To want each other.

And now, it was finally time. To seal their vows in the age-old way.

Yes, in some cynical corner of his mind, Justin was more than aware that such wild flights of imagination, such absurd leaps of logic, were ridiculous in the extreme.

But right then, with Katie soft and willing in his arms, he believed them, anyway.

And that was the greatest miracle of all: that right then, Justin Caldwell *believed.*

He captured her other breast in his mouth and she groaned low in her throat, her body arching, offering him more. He moaned in answer, his fingers skimming the creamy flesh of her belly, dipping lower…

"Oh! Oh, yes…"

He murmured soothing, ardent sounds against her breast and he continued to explore the warm, soft curves and hollows of her body.

The pajamas tied at the waist.

Easily dispensed with. He pulled on the tail of the little bow she'd made and the bow gave way. It was a simple matter then to slip his hand beneath the worn flannel…

She gasped and clutched his head tighter against

her breast. He drew on her nipple more strongly and her hips began to rock against the lumpy mattress. She moaned, her fingers loosening in his hair. He lifted his head enough to glance up at her sweet face as she tossed her head on the blankets, her dark hair, alive with static, clinging where it rubbed.

He stroked the inward curve of her smooth belly, dipping a finger into her navel.

Her breath caught. She made small, hungry mewing sounds. He wanted to kiss those sounds from her lips.

And he did, letting go of her breast and taking her mouth once more, as his hand slid upward, to caress the sleek flesh high on her stomach, to clasp the side of her slim waist, to trace the lower curve of her ribs where they arched above her midsection.

By then, the sounds from her throat were pleading ones.

He dared to ease his fingers beneath the flannel again, to stroke the silky curls at the place where her soft thighs joined. She stiffened, but only for a moment.

Soon enough, her hips began rocking again.

He dipped farther down, parting the soft curls, easing a finger into her moist cleft. She bucked hard against his hand and he cupped her, steadying her as he kissed her deeply, his own body aching with the need to be buried within her.

No.

Not yet. This part was for her—and, yes, for him, too.

He wanted to feel her give herself over; he wanted to give her satisfaction first, before he took his own.

Right then, as he stroked her, as her body moved in rhythm to his intimate touch, it came to him. Like a blinding, painful light switching on in velvet darkness, he realized…

It wasn't going to happen.

Ridiculous fantasies of past lives aside, crazy dreams of a mail-order marriage come true to the contrary, he wasn't going to have her fully.

Even tonight she couldn't be really his.

He had no condoms and she didn't, either.

This. Right now. Her body moving in hungry yearning under his hand, her mouth eager and soft against his own, this was all he could have.

All he would ever have.

He groaned in agony at the thought and pressed himself, hard and aching, against the side of her thigh.

She clung to him, whimpering, as he slipped that finger inside again, even daring to ease in another, stretching her a little. She was tight and very wet.

So good, so right.

He realized he was whispering the words against her parted lips. "So good, so right…"

"Yes," she answered, soft and sweet and oh-so-willing. "Oh, Justin, yes…."

Her hips moved faster. He followed the cues her body gave him, finding the nub of her greatest pleasure, rubbing it, stroking it….

She said his name again against his mouth, on a low breath of yearning and building excitement.

And then he felt it. The soft pulsing beneath his stroking finger, the silky spurt of wetness as she came…

She cried out and he caught that cry, kissing her deeply, as below the tiny, hot, wet pulsing continued.

In the end, her body went loose and boneless. She gave a final, gentle sigh.

His body *hurt*. He ached for more, and yet…

It was good. Better than good, just to be here, in this old bed with her, to know she'd hit the peak and loved every minute of it, that he had done that for her.

She lifted a lazy hand to stroke the side of his face and he raised his head to look down into her shining eyes.

"Oh, Justin…" Her sweet mouth trembled on a smile.

He kissed the tip of her nose. And then, slowly, reluctantly, he took his hand from that wet, hot secret place between her sleek thighs and smoothed her pajama bottoms to cover her to the waist. He took the sides of her top, one and then the other, bringing them together, proceeding to slip the buttons back into their too-loose holes.

She caught his hand. "Oh, don't…"

He gave her a dark look. "Katie. We've got to be careful. You have to know. That was as far as we can go."

She only looked at him, eyes dazed, mouth swollen from his kisses, cheeks flushed: a woman more than willing to go on from here.

Willing? Hell. Eager.

Ready.

For him.

With a low groan, he fell back on the bed, throwing his arm across his eyes, ordering the bulge in his jeans to subside.

*Now.*

It didn't happen—which hardly surprised him.

The bed shifted as she sat up. He dared to steal a peek at her from under the shadow of his arm.

She was taking off her pajama top.

"What the hell are you doing?"

Her high, cute breasts bounced as she tossed that top aside. "Getting undressed." It flew over and hooked on the vanity mirror. "And so should you. Now."

He shouldn't be peeking. He should cover his eyes again.

But somehow, he couldn't. The bulge in his pants only got bigger as she slithered out of the pajama bottoms and tossed them over to land with the top.

Now, all she had left were those thick, gray socks of hers. Her skin seemed to glow in the dimness, rich as vanilla ice cream, but with a pearly kind of luster, too. The sable hair between her soft thighs was shiny with moisture.

And the scent of her…ripe. Purely sexual. The scent of a woman aroused and satisfied. It clung to his hand.

Exercising every last shred of will he possessed, he held back a groan.

This was not going well.

She got rid of the socks, ripping them off, one and then the other, and tossing them to the rag rug beside the bed. "Okay, Justin. I'm naked."

As if he didn't know. As if every inch of him wasn't painfully aware.

He pressed his arm hard against his eyes. He was not going to look. Not again. No matter what.

She spoke again. "Justin. I want to get into bed. But you're on the blankets…"

"Uh. Right. Sorry." He shut his eyes tight and jumped from the bed, letting out another groan as his jeans dug in at the crucial spot.

He stood there, eyes shut, body rigid and burning, facing away from her. Behind him, he heard the covers rustling.

"Safe to look now," she said at last, her tone just slightly teasing. "I'm all covered up."

He yanked his sweater down low over his jeans, to mask the clear evidence that his body refused to be ruled by his mind. And then, with a deep breath and a silent vow that he would not climb onto that bed with her again, he turned to face her.

She sat against the pillows, shining dark hair soft and wild on her satiny shoulders, the blankets pulled up to cover those tempting breasts, looking achingly sweet, and not quite as confident as a moment ago. "I…well, I can't help it. It's crazy, but I almost feel as if we *are* married, you know? As if making love with you is the most natural, *right* thing for us to be doing."

It was exactly what he'd been thinking not long before.

*But so what?* his cynical side reminded him. *So damn what?* They *weren't* married. They would never be married. In a week she would hate him and know him for the enemy he was and had always been.

And, all sentimental talk of "feeling" married aside, they had no protection. They shouldn't have gone as far as they had.

And they damn well weren't going to go any further. "Katie." His voice was rough. Pained. Pushed out through his clutching throat, threaded with his own frustration. "We can't. You know we can't."

She picked at a thread on the velvet patchwork spread, eyes cast down, lashes wisps of silk against her cheeks. "You're right. I know…" She looked up. Those honey-brown eyes captured him, held him—a prisoner of his own burning need for her. "But couldn't we just…" She paused to swallow, convulsively—and then didn't seem to be able to go on.

"Couldn't we, *what?*" he demanded way too gruffly.

She swallowed again and licked those soft lips with a nervous pink tongue—an unintentionally provocative action that inflicted yet another blow to his barely held self-control.

"Well," she suggested, all wide eyes and innocence, "you could put on those black sweats you sleep in. I'll put my pajamas back on, too. You can…come to bed with me."

"Come to bed with you." There was nothing—*nothing*—he'd rather do. And it was exactly what he was *not* going do. "Katie—"

She cut him off before he could tell her no. "Oh, listen. Please…"

"We can't—"

"No, see. Just listen. We won't do anything more. I promise…to be good."

They shared a look—hot and hungry, crackling with need.

And then, out of nowhere, she laughed, a happy, startled, captivating trill of sound.

That laugh was infectious. He laughed, too—and then he stopped himself and glared at her. "What the hell are we laughing at?"

"Well, Justin, it's only…me, sitting here naked. Promising not to try anymore to seduce *you*. Who would have guessed *that* would happen?"

He only looked at her, making no attempt to smile. He was thinking that she'd been seducing him since the first moment he saw her, when Caleb introduced them and he got his first look into those wide, soft brown eyes.

There was just something about her. She got to him in ways he'd never been gotten to before.

"Please," she said, so sweetly.

"Hell," he replied.

"Please," she said, once more.

And once again, there was no stopping the wrong words from escaping his mouth.

"Put on those damn pajamas," he growled. "I'll be right back."

## Chapter Nine

"Spooning," Katie whispered.

They lay on their sides, her slim back tucked into him, her legs cradled on his, his arm across her waist. He nuzzled her hair, cuddled her closer, in spite of the fact that holding her tighter only aroused him more.

"Yes," she said. "Spooning."

"What in hell are you talking about?"

She chuckled. The sweet sound vibrated through him. "What we're doing, tucked in this bed together, fully clothed, with you curved all around me. We're spooning."

He grunted, smoothed a wild coil of fragrant hair away from his mouth, and muttered, "We're driving me crazy, that's what we're doing."

"Hmm," she said, and wiggled her bottom against him.

He took a slow breath. "That was completely un-called for."

"Sorry."

"Liar."

"But seriously, courting couples used to do this, in the old days...lie down together, with their clothes on, tucked up nice and cozy, like spoons in a drawer. Thus, spooning."

"Spooning." He laid his hand over hers, stroking the back of it, until she opened her fingers and he slid his between. She tucked their joined fists against her soft, flannel-covered breasts. He growled in her ear. "Frankly, I'd rather be shtupping."

She giggled. "I don't believe you said that."

"The truth hurts. Let me tell you, it really, *really* hurts."

She elbowed him lightly. "I'll distract you."

"Don't worry, you already are."

"I mean, from your, er, pain."

"Oh. That. Good luck."

"Back to spooning... Soldiers have done it, far back in history, spooning in the trenches to ward off the cold on a freezing night before a big battle. They'd keep warm using each other's body heat."

"Speaking of which, it's too damn hot in here." He pulled his hand from hers and readjusted the covers, pushing them down on his side.

"Umm." She wiggled in against him again. "Better?"

It was agony, but at the same time... "Yeah."

"Give me your hand back, please." He obliged. She tucked it under her soft chin. "Yes," she said on a gentle sigh. "This is nice…"

*Nice* wasn't exactly the word for it.

Spooning.

Never in a million and a half years would he have pictured himself, lying here, *spooning* Katie Fenton.

But he *was* lying here, with her sweet-scented softness plastered all along the front of him, holding her tight, both of them covered in clothing from neck to ankle. He *was* lying here, never wanting to let her go.

He knew he'd never get any sleep like this. But he closed his eyes, anyway.

He woke abruptly as Katie threw back the covers and jumped from the bed.

He sat up. She was already past the rope he'd dropped last night, racing for the door to the front reception room.

He raked the hair back from his forehead. "Huh, wha—?"

She sent him a dazzling smile and hauled open the door. "The phone's ringing."

It rang again as she slipped through the doorway.

Katie picked up the phone in midring. "Hello?" No one spoke. She asked again, more urgently, "Hello?"

"Katie, darling? Oh, thank goodness."

She felt the huge smile burst across her face. "Addy."

"You're there…you're safe?"

"Oh, Addy. Yes. I'm fine. Justin and I got stuck here, at the museum. But we're okay. We're safe. Buttercup's even okay—though she's getting pretty cranky, trapped in the shed out back with only hay to eat."

"You're safe." The relief in Addy's dear voice was achingly clear. "We've been so worried...."

"I'm fine. Really. And so is Justin. Don't worry anymore. Everything's great, but what about you? And Caleb? And Riley?"

"Safe. We're all safe." A gentle chuckle followed. "Riley made it home from the hall before the snow got too bad. Caleb and I and Mr. Sy Goodwin got stuck in that office in town."

"The ski resort office?"

"You know Caleb. Sy's visiting from Billings. He expressed interest in the project and Caleb wanted to take him right over there to show him what a good investment he'd be making. I tagged along. By the time we realized we needed to get home, it was too late. But we all three made it back to the hall, and spent Sunday and Monday and three endless, uncomfortable nights there, with the others who didn't make it home. It was an adventure, I'll tell you."

"Where are you now?"

"The snowplows started working last evening. Thunder Canyon Road was cleared by seven this morning."

Katie looked at the clock on the wall—ten thirty-five. "So you're at the Lazy D?"

"That's right. Home safe and sound."

Katie clutched the phone tighter. "Oh, I'm so relieved. I was worried about everyone."

"Nothing to worry about. We're all safe, and Caleb wants to talk to you."

"Okay, I—"

Before she finished her sentence, Caleb's deep voice was blustering in her ear. "Katie. Honey, you're all right?"

Katie smiled all the wider. "I'm fine. Really. Safe and warm, and we had food to eat, sandwiches left by the Historical Society ladies. We're pretty tired of ham and cheese, but it all worked out. Truly."

"Justin Caldwell?"

The sound of his name on Caleb's lips made her blush, for some silly reason—or maybe it was the memory of last night. "He's here, with me. Safe. I promise."

"All right, then. Katie, honey, you'll be out of there in no time. I'm making a few calls to see that plow gets to you right away."

"Caleb, that's really not necessary. We're perfectly safe and we can wait."

Caleb wouldn't hear of that. "I'm getting you out of there, and I'm doing it quick. Just sit tight now and hold on." He spoke to someone—Addy, no doubt—on his end of the line. "Addy wants you to come on out to the ranch for dinner tonight. We'll celebrate how we all got through the worst blizzard of the century—so far, anyway—safe and sound. She says to invite Caldwell, too. Can't have an out-of-towner thinking we don't know how to treat a guest."

He chuckled again. "Especially one who happens to be my business partner."

Nice idea, she thought. *Lovely* idea. "I'll ask him."

"Good. I'm going to let you go now. I want you to call me if that plow doesn't show up in the next hour."

She wouldn't, of course. She and Justin could wait as long as it took. But Caleb always enjoyed pulling strings for the people who mattered to him. "Thanks, Caleb. I love you—Addy, too."

He made the usual, gruff, blustering sounds. "Well, now, who's my girl?"

"*I* am. Always. Bye now."

She hung up and turned to find Justin leaning in the doorway to the central room, one bare foot crossed lazily over the other. Her heart set to pounding and her breath caught at the sight of him—at the memory of last night that seemed to shimmer in the air between them.

"That was Caleb and Addy." She sounded breathless. Probably because she *was*. "They were worried. I told them we were fine. And they said everyone else is safe, too."

"Good." He straightened from his easy slouch and came toward her, the predatory gleam in his eyes causing her knees to go weak and something low in her belly to go soft as melting butter.

She suffered dual urges—to back away from him; and to throw herself against him and lift up her mouth. In the end, she did neither. She held her ground, waiting, as he stalked toward her.

He reached her, his eyes still burning into hers.

A nervous laugh escaped her. "Justin, you look so…" The sentence trailed off. She didn't know quite how to finish it.

He lifted a hand. With a light finger, he guided a stray coil of hair behind her ear. A little shiver went through her. "Cold?"

"No. No, not at all. Justin, are you okay?"

His hand dropped to his side and he stepped back. "So, today we're really getting out of here."

She nodded. "If we're lucky, the plow should be here in the next few hours."

He turned from her, abruptly. "Let's get the coffee going."

She caught his arm. "Justin…"

He swung back, his eyes dark. Turbulent. His bicep was rock-hard with tension beneath her hand. "What?"

She let go, fast. "I…well, you almost seem angry. I just don't get it."

He kept staring at her, giving her that strange, hot, dark *devouring* look, for an endless, tense moment and then…

His eyes changed. Softened. His wonderful, sensual mouth went soft, too. "Hell." And he reached out and pulled her into his strong arms, squeezing the breath right out of her.

"Justin, what—?"

"I don't want to lose you." The rough, whispered words seemed dredged up from the deepest part of him.

"Oh, Justin." She held on, tight as he was holding her. "You won't. Of course, you won't."

A low, pained sound came from him and he crushed her so close, as if he would push himself right into her, meld their separate bodies into one undividable whole.

An image flashed into her mind: of the boy he once was, a boy all alone when he shouldn't have been, standing at a wide window, watching the snow come down, wondering what was going to happen to him.

"You can count on me," she whispered, meaning it with every fiber of her being. "You can hold on to me. I'll always be here."

He held her close for an endless moment more and then, with a shuddering sigh, his arms relaxed. She raised her head to meet his eyes and a rueful half smile lifted a corner of his mouth.

"Damned if I wasn't kind of getting to like it here."

She surged up, pressed a kiss on his beard-shadowed jaw. "Me, too. Oh, Justin...me, too."

Over morning coffee and the inevitable sandwiches, she relayed Addy's dinner invitation.

His eyes shifted away for a split second, and then he shook his head. "Wish I could. But I need to get back to Bozeman, ASAP. In my business, there are a hundred issues to deal with on a daily basis. I've been away since Saturday morning and that's three days too long."

She set down her stale sandwich and resisted the urge to work on him to stay. The guy had a demanding job and if they were going to get anywhere together, she'd have to learn to live with that—and on second thought, there were no *ifs* about it. The way he'd held her, as if he'd never let her go, out in the reception room a while ago, had banished all doubts on that score.

"I'm disappointed," she said, matter-of-factly. "But I do understand."

"Will you thank Adele for the invitation—and express my regrets?"

"You know I will—and it could be tough to get home at this point. You realize that?" Well, okay, she couldn't help hoping that maybe bad road conditions would keep him in town tonight, after all. He could stay at her place.

They could catch up on their spooning.

She might even make a quick trip to the drugstore, take care of the contraception problem. She'd never bought a condom in her life and old Mr. Dodson, the pharmacist, might give her the lifted eyebrow when she plunked the box down at the cash register counter. But it would definitely be worth the slight embarrassment, to make tonight extra special, a night to remember.

Always…

But then Justin said, "It's not even twenty miles. And by later today, at least, I'm sure they'll have the highway cleared."

He was probably right. Darn it.

The plow came within the hour. By then, Caleb had called a second time to tell her not to worry about Buttercup. A couple of hands would be over a little later with the snowblower and other necessary equipment to free the mare from the shed out back. Emelda

Ross had called, as well, just to check and see that Katie was all right.

Katie and Justin, still dressed in their rummage sale clothes, bundled in the coats and gloves they'd arrived in, shovels in hand, waited on the porch as the plow lumbered up the street. It turned into the museum parking lot and kept on coming, right up to the steps. Katie waved at the driver, a local man whose wife and kids paid frequent visits to the library, and shouted, "Thanks!"

The driver gave her a wave in return and then backed to the street again. The plow, which had already made the Elk Avenue curve, headed east at a crawl, toward what was known as New Town, clearing the high white drifts into yet higher piles at the sides of the street as it went.

Justin turned to her. "Well. What next?"

A dragging feeling of sadness engulfed her: for all they had shared in the dim rooms behind them, for the uncertain future—which, she told herself firmly, wasn't uncertain at all.

She and the man beside her had found something special. Nothing could change that. "Where's your car parked?" she asked with a cheery smile.

"In the lot behind the town hall."

"It's not far, and mine's there, too. Let's get the steps cleared off and put the shovels away and then we'll start walking."

All along Main Street, folks were out with their shovels. The roar of snowblowers filled the icy air.

People called out and waved as Katie and Justin walked by.

"Katie, how you doin'?"

"Some storm, eh?"

"Talk about your New Year's surprise!"

"Come on. This is nothin'. Five or six feet. Piece a cake."

"And they say it's turning warm right away. In the fifties by Friday. What do you think of that?"

They waved back and called greetings and when they reached the hall, they found the front steps already cleared and the driveway to the back parking lot passable, as well.

They went in the front to ask after the things they'd left behind the night of the storm. Rhonda Culpepper, well past sixty with a white streak in her improbably black hair, waited at her usual post behind the reception desk.

Rhonda greeted Katie and nodded at Justin and announced with a wink, "I'll bet I know what you two are after." She bent down behind the desk and came up with Katie's purse and Justin's briefcase, phone and keys, along with a big bag for each of them filled with their own clothes and shoes. "Have I got everything?"

"Looks like it. Thanks, Rhonda."

"Always glad to help."

They went down a side hall and out a door at the back. A couple of guys were at work there, clearing the snow between the vehicles so people could get them out. Katie exchanged greetings with the men and then Justin asked which car was hers.

She pointed at the silver-gray Suburban, near where the men were working. "In a few minutes they'll have me dug out."

"Let's get the snow off the roof and the windshield cleared, then," he suggested.

She caught his hand. Even through their heavy gloves, she felt his warmth. Her pulse quickened. "It's okay. Doug and Cam will help me." She gestured at the two busily shoveling men.

"You're sure?"

"Absolutely. Where are you parked?"

His black Escalade was near the edge of the lot, not far from the drive that led around to the front. The snow had already been shoveled away around it.

She helped him knock some of the snow off the roof and the hood and he got inside and turned the vehicle on, ducking back out with a scraper. He set to work. She went on tiptoe and pushed more snow off the Escalade's roof as he cleared the windshield.

It wasn't all that long before he had the wipers going and he was ready to head out.

He cast a glance toward Cam and Doug, still shoveling away between the snow-covered cars and pickups. "Come here." He grabbed her hand and towed her to the back of the Escalade, where they were out of sight of the working men. She went eagerly into the warm circle of his arms.

"Time to get out of here." His breath came out on a cloud.

"Drive safely. I want you back soon. Very, very soon…"

By way of answer, he bent and pressed his lips—cold on the outside, so warm within—to hers.

The icy day, the growls of snowblowers on Main Street, the scraping of shovels on the frozen blacktop a few feet away—all of that faded to nothing. There was only Justin, his arms tight and cherishing around her, his mouth claiming hers in a bone-melting kiss.

With a regretful growl low in his throat, he lifted his head. "I'll call you."

She let out a laugh. "Good luck with that. You don't even have my number."

"Katie, you're the town librarian and you're like a daughter to Caleb Douglas, who happens to be a colleague of mine. I don't think you'll be that hard to track down. Plus, I'd bet the last strip mall I built that you've got a listed number."

"Now, how did you know that?"

"You're the listed-number type."

She gave him a frown. "That's good, right?"

He kissed her nose, her cheeks and even her chin, his lips warm now against her cold skin. Then he pulled away enough to look at her, a deep look, a look she couldn't quite read. "I have to go." His arms fell away and he turned toward the driver's door.

She followed, already missing him, feeling bereft. He climbed up into the seat and shut the door. She went around the front of the vehicle to the other side, getting out of his way.

He saluted her—a gloved hand to his forehead. She mimicked the gesture. And then he was backing out, turning to get the right angle, and rolling forward. She watched as the big, black SUV disappeared around the side of the town hall, her heart pounding hard and heavy as lead beneath her breastbone.

She knew he would call her. Hadn't he just told her he would? Still, she had the strangest, scariest feeling right then that she would never see him again.

## Chapter Ten

Dinner at the Lazy D was a festive affair. Adele had the cook prepare a juicy prime rib and Tess Little-hawk, the ranch's longtime housekeeper, set the long table in the formal dining room with the best china and crystal.

Riley, who'd been out earlier checking the stock, came in from his own place a half a mile from the main house to join them, his dark hair slicked back, wet from the shower he must have just taken.

"I was the lucky one," he said, smoothing his linen napkin on his lap and sparing a wink of greeting for Katie. "Safe and sound at my place before things got too rough."

Sy Goodwin, a feed-store owner and family man who'd decided to stay the night before heading back to his wife and four kids in Billings, laughed with

Caleb and Adele over their shared "ordeal" in the hall—especially Sunday morning, when most of the others were suffering from an excess of beer the day before.

"A number of extremely discouraging words were exchanged," Goodwin reported, his expression jokingly solemn, a definite gleam in his eye.

The creases in Caleb's nut-brown face etched all the deeper as he let out his big, boisterous laugh. "I tell you, Katie, a bottle of aspirin that first day was worth its weight in gold."

Sy laughed, too. "And anyone with a box of Alka-Seltzer could have gotten a fortune for it."

Adele and Caleb agreed that Sy wasn't exaggerating.

Caleb asked, a little too meaningfully as far as Katie was concerned, "And what about you and Justin? Stuck there in that musty old museum with nothing but mining equipment and Indian artifacts for company."

Adele was shaking her head. "What *did* you do for all that time?"

*We kissed,* Katie thought. *Forever. We spooned. All night. And I dropped in at State Street Drugs this afternoon and bought myself a box of condoms.* Mr. Dodson hadn't even batted an eye when she plunked it down on the counter.

She said, offhand as she could make it, "Oh, we found some books and board games in the storage room. We managed to occupy ourselves."

Addy clucked her tongue and sent Katie a sly look. "A handsome guy, that Justin."

Katie put on her sweetest smile. "Yes. He is. Very."

Adele added, "I do wish he'd been able to stay and join us tonight."

"He had to get back," Katie said. "Business, you know."

"Yeah," Caleb agreed. "That man's a real go-getter. Started from nothing and now he's the biggest developer in western Montana—and not even thirty-five yet." Those devilish green eyes of his were twinkling. "And our Katie's gone and married him."

Addy and Riley shared a glance and Sy Goodwin looked confused.

Adele had to explain to him about the mail-order bride reenactment they'd missed when they went down to the ski resort office.

"We heard after we got back to the hall that it was quite an event, that marriage of yours," said Caleb. "Heard some old character named Green stepped up to play the preacher. Got right into the part. Even called himself 'Reverend.'"

"Yep," Katie agreed, keeping it light, but thinking of Justin. Of his low, teasing voice through the darkness that night they'd talked and talked. Of his kiss. Of his hands on her body. She should have gotten his number. But no. He'd said he'd call. And of course he would. "That 'wedding' was…really something."

Maybe tonight, she thought. At least by tomorrow…

The talk moved on to other subjects. After coffee and dessert, Caleb and Addy urged her to stay. They didn't want her driving home on the icy roads in the dark.

She said she really had to get back. The roads to town had been cleared and salted and the snow hadn't started up again. She'd be just fine.

It was after eleven when she let herself into her two-story farmhouse-style Victorian on Cedar Street.

She'd been home earlier, after Justin left her in the town hall parking lot, and she'd turned up the thermostat then, so the house was cozy-warm and welcoming. Switching on lamps as she went, she headed for the phone in the kitchen in back, where she found the message light on her machine glowing a steady red.

No one had called.

He didn't call Wednesday morning, either. Katie went to the library at nine and jumped every time the phone rang, though there was really no reason he'd call her at work when all he had to do was look up her home number in the book.

Still, whenever the phone rang, her heart would race and the clerk would answer.

And it wouldn't be him.

Emelda, who put in a lot of volunteer hours at the library, arrived at two. "It's going to be fifty degrees today, can you believe it?" she marveled as she peeled off her muffler and hung up her heavy coat. "Snow's already melting. It'll be gone in no time if this keeps up." She clucked her tongue and got to work shelving some new novels Katie had waiting.

At three, Emelda took over the check-out desk so

the clerk, Lindy Peters, could have a break. The phone rang just as Lindy left the desk. Katie raced over and grabbed it on the second ring, though Emelda was moving down the counter toward it.

"Thunder Canyon Public Library," Katie answered, absurdly breathless. "May I help you?"

It was only someone wanting the library hours for the week. Katie repeated them and said goodbye.

Emelda shook her silver-gray head. "I swear you are jumpy as a frog on a hot rock today. I would have gotten that."

Katie hardly heard her. Her mind was full of Justin. What was he doing now? Had he gotten back to Bozeman safely? Well, of course he had. And it had barely been twenty-four hours since he left her at the town hall—well, okay, twenty-six hours, thirty-plus minutes, to be more exact. Not that long, not really. No doubt he had a mountain of work to catch up on. He probably wouldn't be able to get away to see her until the weekend. He'd be calling—soon—to set something up.

"Katie? Did you hear a single word I said?"

"Oh. Emelda. Sorry, I…" She was saved from having to make some lame excuse for her distracted behavior when a little girl with a towering stack of picture books, her mother right behind her, stepped up to the counter.

After that, Katie managed to keep herself from rushing to grab the phone every time it rang.

Besides, by then she was feeling more and more certain that Justin would be calling her house, not the library. There was probably a message waiting for her at home right now.

When she got home at five-fifteen there were two messages, but neither was from Justin.

She simply had to stop obsessing over this. He'd said he'd call and he would. Justin was an honest man.

That night she hosted the Historical Society meeting at her house. As she served up the coffee and cookies and listened to everyone bemoan the storm that had ruined their museum reception, and trade news on Ben Saunders's rapidly improving health, she couldn't help expecting the phone to ring.

It didn't. Not that night, not Thursday morning, not during her prelunch hours at the library, either.

She met Addy for their usual Thursday lunch date at the Hitching Post. Addy mentioned that she thought Katie seemed distracted.

Katie met Addy's eyes across the table and longed to tell her everything—of the magic time she'd known with Justin when they were marooned in the museum, of the shattering beauty of the one night she'd spent in his arms.

Of how she couldn't stop longing, every second of the day, for his call.

But no. It was all too new. She didn't want to share what she was feeling with anyone. Not yet. Not until...

Well, soon. But not now.

She reassured Addy that she was fine.

And then Justin didn't call the rest of the day, or in the evening, either.

By Friday morning she was beginning to wonder if something really might have happened to him, if he'd had some kind of accident on the way home to Bozeman. Whatever had kept him from calling her, she prayed he was all right.

She pored over the special edition of the *Thunder Canyon Nugget* that had come out Wednesday. It was chock-full of great stories of how folks had weathered the big storm. Two storm-related accidents were reported. One had occurred after the roads were cleared, when a pickup going too fast rolled on Thunder Canyon Road. The other concerned a high-schooler who'd driven his snowmobile into a tree while the snow was still falling on Sunday afternoon. Injuries were surprisingly minor in both cases. She found no mention of any accident on the road to Bozeman, nothing about a black Escalade or an out-of-towner named Caldwell.

Before she left for the library, she called Bozeman information. His home phone wasn't listed. But they did have a number for Red Rock Developers. She dialed it and a service picked up. The offices opened at nine. She could leave her number and Mr. Caldwell's secretary would get back to her during business hours.

"Uh, no thanks. I'll call later."

She hung up and considered calling Caleb, asking him if maybe he had Justin's home number. But she found herself hesitating to do that. Caleb would be curious. He'd tease her about her "groom," and ask her why she thought she needed his number. And then Caleb would tell Adele that Katie was trying to get ahold of Justin—and Addy would tell Caleb how distracted Katie had been at lunch the day before…

Oh, not right now, she thought. She wanted to find out how Justin was, wanted to *talk* to him, wanted to be reassured that everything was all right, with him and between the two of them, before she said anything to Caleb or Addy.

She went to work and tried to keep her mind on her job, a difficult task when every thought kept tracking right back around to Justin. Where was he? Was he okay? Why hadn't he called?

By lunchtime, after Lindy had asked her twice what was wrong with her and Emelda had expressed concern over whether she might be coming down with something, Katie realized she had to snap out of it.

Worrying about Justin wasn't going to do anybody any good. She'd track him down that evening, one way or another. Until then, she was keeping her thoughts strictly on her work.

At four-fifteen, the kids started arriving for Emelda's story hour, which started at four-thirty. They all gathered around the low round table in the center of the children's section, where Emelda would keep them spellbound with fairy tales and stories by the best contemporary children's authors—and sometimes true-life accounts from Montana history.

Cameron Stevenson, one of the two men Katie and Justin had found shoveling out the town hall parking lot on Tuesday, brought his seven-year-old, Erik, as always. Often the parents would leave their kids and come back at five-thirty to collect them.

Not Cam. The tall, athletic auburn-haired teacher

was a single dad and he took fatherhood seriously. He stuck around, even though he coached at the high school and would have to rush back there the minute the story hour ended to get his team ready for the evening's home game. As he waited, he read sports magazines from the periodicals section and browsed the fiction stacks.

After five, as Katie was wrapping things up for the day, Cam wandered over to her workstation at the central reference counter and he and Katie chatted about nothing in particular: how good the varsity basketball team was looking this year and how Cam and Erik had barely made it home Saturday before the snow shut them in.

Cam joked that he'd heard how she and her "groom" had been stuck at the museum alone for the duration. "Some honeymoon, huh?" he asked with an easy grin.

"It was…quite an experience," she replied in a library-level whisper, mentally congratulating herself on how offhand she sounded. "Poor Buttercup."

"That old mare of Caleb's, you mean?"

She nodded. "The old sweetheart was stuck out in the shed all that time, no exercise and nothing but hay to…" She didn't finish.

How could she? Her throat had clamped tight. Joy and relief went exploding through her.

Justin!

He must have just come in. He stood over by the check-out counter, wearing a sweater that matched his eyes and a gorgeous coffee-brown suede jacket. He was scanning the room.

He spotted her. Her heart froze in midbeat and then started galloping. Somehow, she managed to lift a hand and wave.

He headed toward her, long strides eating up the all-weather gray carpet under his boots. She was vaguely aware that Cam had turned to see what—or who—had stolen the words right out of her mouth.

"I had a feeling I might find you here," Justin said.

Good gravy, he really was the best-looking man in the whole of Montana! She had to swallow to make her throat relax before she could speak. "Uh. Good guess. And, um, great to see you."

It was the understatement of the decade.

She collected her scattered wits enough to introduce him to Cam. The two men exchanged greetings and then Cam left them alone.

The second the coach was out of earshot, Justin asked low, "When do you finish here?"

She ordered her crazy heart to stop racing. "Give me a minute. I'm almost ready to go."

As they passed the check-out desk, Lindy called out, "Have a nice night." Plump and pretty and very curious, the clerk gave them a big grin and wiggled her eyebrows at Katie.

Katie, getting the message, stopped to introduce them.

"Terrific to meet you!" Lindy enthused. Sheesh. She was practically drooling.

Then again, who could blame her?

Justin made a few cordial noises and at last they were out of there.

They walked down the library steps into a winter sunset. The cloudless sky was shades of salmon above the white-topped mountains and the melting snow at their feet sent rivulets trickling, down the steps, along the parking lot. A hundred miniature streams gleamed in the gathering dark.

She sent a quick glance toward the silent man at her side. He hadn't touched her—hadn't taken her arm. She longed to take his, but didn't feel comfortable enough with him at that moment, with the way he'd popped up out of nowhere, with the strange, shadowed look in his eyes and the hard set to his square jaw.

"Where's your car?" he asked flatly when they reached the big, black Escalade.

"I walked. It's only a few blocks and it was nice to get out." She almost said more. Meaningless chatter. About the warming trend. About how she liked to walk whenever the weather permitted. But she didn't. His eyes didn't invite chitchat. "Justin, what—?"

He cut in before she finished. "Who was that guy you were talking to inside?"

Her heart warmed. So that was the problem. He was *jealous.* "Cam? He's only a friend. Honestly. A friend…"

His mouth twisted into something meant to look like a smile. "Not that I had any damn right to ask."

She looked at him levelly. "If you were wondering, then I'm *glad* you asked. It's important that we both feel we can say whatever's on our minds."

"Is it?" He lifted a dark brow at her.

She blinked. "Now what is *that* supposed to mean?"

He shrugged. "Nothing."

Untrue and she knew it. It was very much *something*. She could see it in his eyes.

But before she could open her mouth to pursue the issue, he spoke again. "Will you have dinner with me?"

There was only one answer to that one. "I'd love to."

"Where would you like to go?"

He sounded so...formal. As if she was some stranger.

It came to her that she didn't want to go and sit in a restaurant with him. Surrounded by other people, she wouldn't feel she could really talk to him. And she needed that, to feel free to talk. This new distance between them scared her a little. She wanted, with all her heart, to bridge it.

And then again, was this feeling of distance really all that surprising? They'd found a rare and thrilling intimacy, just the two of them, in the museum. But she had to remember that they'd known each other less than a week. The attraction had been immediate and the forced proximity had made it possible for them to grow close very fast.

And then he'd returned to his life and she'd gone back to hers.

No. She had to expect that things would be a little awkward, now they found themselves face-to-face again at last.

She intended to eliminate the awkwardness, to

break down any and all barriers between them. That would be easier if they were alone.

"Tell you what? Let's just go to my place. How about fried chicken and oven-browned red potatoes, would that be all right?"

He frowned. "You're sure?"

She stepped back, a half laugh escaping her. "Justin. What's not to be sure of?"

He hesitated a moment longer. But finally, he agreed. "Well, all right, then. Let's go."

## Chapter Eleven

"**B**ig place," Justin said, when Katie ushered him into a high-ceilinged foyer, where a walnut staircase rose gracefully from the far end, curving upward toward the second floor.

She set her purse on the long marble table by the door and turned to knock the breath out of him with a glowing smile. "It was in bad shape when I bought it, but I've had a lot of work done. It was built in 1910, by the owner of the town dry goods store. Cedar Street used to be where all the town merchants lived. A lot of them were well-to-do."

"Clearly." Beneath his boots, the fine, old wood of the parquet floor gave off a polished shine in the glow from the antique light fixture overhead. Carved walnut moldings crowned the walls.

She teased, "Take a good look around. Just in case

you're thinking of making me an offer." He met those brown eyes again and a shock of sensual awareness ricocheted through him.

He wanted to grab her and carry her up the curving staircase, to find a nice, big bed up there and never let her out of it. "I'm tempted," he muttered, and they both knew damn well he wasn't talking about her house.

He ached. All over. His damn skin felt too tight. He had only himself to blame for the state he was in. Not only for starting up with her in the first place, but for not taking care of his physical needs since he'd left her on Tuesday.

There were a couple of women he knew: willing, bright, beautiful women, who didn't expect—or even want—anything beyond a nice evening and a good time in bed. But he hadn't been able to make himself pick up the phone and call one of them.

His body burned for the satisfaction he hadn't allowed himself to take four nights ago in that big, old bed in the museum. But he'd done nothing to ease the ache. The thought of touching some other woman for the sake of a much-needed release…

It made him feel vaguely ill.

His mistake. To add to all the others. He should have at least taken a few minutes in the shower to get the edge off, but he hadn't even had sense enough to do that.

Somehow, he couldn't. He wanted Katie. His *body* wanted Katie. Only Katie.

Though he knew damn well he was never going to have her.

"Oh, Justin..." Her voice was so soft, like the rest of her. His arms itched to hold her. With monumental effort, he kept his hands at his sides. She seemed to shake herself and then, shyly, she offered, "May I take your jacket?"

He shrugged out of it and handed it over. She hung it on the antique claw-footed rack by the door, along with her heavy coat. Then she turned to him again, those amber eyes alight, her smile so bright it could chase away the darkness of the blackest night.

Damn. He was gone. Gone, gone, gone. He kept trying to remember why he'd come here, what he needed to say to her. He should say it.

And go.

But he said nothing as she gestured toward a door at the back, past the foot of that impressive staircase. "This way..." He fell in behind her and she led him to a big kitchen with acres of granite-topped counters and cherrywood cabinets fronted in beveled glass. "Have a seat." She nodded toward the cherry table in the breakfast area. "I'll get the dinner started."

He didn't want to sit there at the table while she bustled around across a jut of counter fifteen feet away. "Let me help."

"Well, sure." She was already at the sink, washing her hands. "If you want to..."

He followed her lead at the sink and then turned to watch her as she tied on an apron, set the oven and began assembling the stuff she needed. He scrubbed the potatoes for her. She cut them into quarters and shook spices on them, then drizzled them with olive oil and stirred them with a wooden spoon.

In spite of the constant, burning ache to grab her and hold her, to kiss her and feel her body go soft and warm and achingly willing against his, in spite of the nagging awareness that he had a grim purpose here and once he accomplished it, he'd have to walk out the door.

And never see her again.

In spite of all of it, a strange sort of peace settled on him, just to be there, with her, in the big, well-appointed kitchen, handing her a spoon or an oven mitt when she asked for it, watching as she prepared their meal.

She battered the chicken, her soft mouth curved in a happy smile. "So. What have you been up to since we broke out of the museum Tuesday?"

He told her how busy he'd been, catching up, getting back on top of the job again. As he talked, she put the chicken on to fry and checked the potatoes.

As she shut the oven door, she asked, "How about some wine?"

"Sounds good."

She went to the chef-quality fridge and brought out a bottle of Pinot Grigio. "Do the honors?"

He opened the wine and poured them each a glass. Then she started on the salad, keeping an eye on the chicken as she worked, and chattering away about the happenings at the library, about the Historical Society meeting she'd held on Wednesday.

"There was much concern over how the storm had ruined our 'wedding reception.' The society members were hoping the event would generate a few generous donations."

"Understandable. Did you tell them how grateful we were that they left all those sandwiches—and what they're collecting for a rummage sale?"

"I didn't," she confessed. "But I guess I should have."

He knocked back a big slug of the excellent wine to keep himself from flinging the glass to the hardwood floor and hauling her into his arms. "Speaking of the rummage sale, I should have brought back that reindeer sweater—not to mention the ugly coat, the jeans and those beat-up sneakers. Sorry. I completely forgot." His mind had been filled with her, with the shining central fact that he'd see her face again. One more time.

Before the end.

"No one's even going to notice that stuff is missing, believe me." She sipped from her own glass—much more daintily than he had. "But if you're feeling *really* guilty, you could make a donation."

"I'll do that."

"It doesn't have to be much. And you'll have the society's undying gratitude."

"Never hurts to build goodwill." He knew he should have choked on those words. After next Tuesday, he'd be the lowest of the low in her eyes. No amount of goodwill would help him then.

She nodded. "Never hurts."

*Never.*

The word got stuck in his mind.

Never to hold her again…

Never to see her smile at him…

Never to look into those wide brown eyes…

He set his wineglass on the counter—a stupid move, and he knew it. With both hands empty, the urge to fill them with her softness was nearly overpowering.

She watched him, her eyes tracking from his face, to his glass and back to his face again. After an endless few seconds of that, she set down her glass, too.

Behind her at the stove, the chicken sizzled in the pan, giving off a mouthwatering, savory smell. The salad sat, half-made, beside her glass.

And he couldn't stop himself from thinking...

If she were someone different, or if he was.

If those vows they'd exchanged Saturday in the town hall had been the real thing.

If she were truly his wife.

This would be their life, here, in this graceful old house, her in her apron, the chicken on the stove, the salad on the counter and the potatoes in the oven.

The two of them, talking about what had happened at work, sharing the little details of their separate days, before they sat down to dinner.

Together.

And later, he'd take her to bed—*their* bed.

He'd hold her and kiss her—kiss every last inch of her. Until she was pliant and heated and ready to have him. He'd enter her slowly, by aching degrees....

"Oh," she said quietly, the word like a yearning sigh between them. "Oh, I did miss you."

It was too much. More than he could bear. His need to touch her took over. He reached out.

With a cry, she swayed toward him. And he wrapped his arms around a miracle.

Katie. Right here. In his hungry arms.

He rained kisses on her soft, flushed cheeks. "I missed you, too. So damn much."

"Oh, me, too. I missed *you*." She let out a giggle and a sweet blush stained her cheeks. "But I already said that, I know I did. I— Oh, Justin. You should kiss me." She tipped up that plump mouth. "You should kiss me right now."

"You're right."

He took her lifted mouth. And she gave it, eagerly, sending a blast of heat exploding through him. She opened for him, so he could plunge his tongue inside and taste her—so sweet, so eager, flavored with wine.

She wore a kitten-soft sweater over a skinny wool skirt. It wasn't enough, to feel her through that fluffy sweater. He eased it up—just a little. He wasn't going to go too far.

He put his hands on the velvety, warm flesh at the small of her back. She moaned into his mouth. He sucked in the sound, breathing in her breath, letting it back out so she could take breath from him.

He muttered her name, between deep kisses on her open lips. "Katie, Katie, Katie…" And his hands…

He couldn't stop them. They wandered up her back, found the place where her bra hooked and eased those tiny hooks apart.

Yes! He brought his hands around, both of them, between them, and he cradled her small, round breasts, groaning at the feel of them, the soft, slight weight against his palms. He scraped her nipples with his thumbs and then caught them, each one, between thumb and forefinger, rolling, pinching a little, just enough to make her push her hips against him, just enough to make her moan.

More.

He had to have more of her.

He had to have *all* of her. Stark need pounded through him as his blood spurted, thick and hot and hungry, through his veins.

He raked that sweater up, losing her mouth so he could kiss her chin, scrape his teeth along her throat, nipping and licking as he went. He nuzzled the fluffy sweater, but only briefly. And then he found her breast.

He latched on and she cried out, clutching his head. He drew on the sweet peak, working his teeth against it, making her cry out again.

As he suckled her, he let his hands slide downward, over the glorious inward curve of her waist and out, along the warm shape of her hips beneath the nubby wool of her skirt.

The skirt was in his way and he wanted it gone.

He grabbed two handfuls of it and eased it upward, over those warm, slim, waiting thighs.

Her panty hose stopped him. His fingers brushed them, and sheer as they were, the slight barrier of nylon reminded him.

He shouldn't be doing this.

He had no damn right to do this.

It took every last ounce of determination he possessed, but he lifted his head. She tried, at first—raising her body to his, pleading sounds rising from her throat—to pull him back to her.

But no.

He couldn't. He had no right to give in to her tender urging.

He lifted his head and her soft hands fell away.

Gently, he smoothed down her skirt as she looked at him, dazed, flushed and dreamy-eyed. "Justin?" She whispered his name on a yearning, slow breath.

He didn't answer. *Couldn't* answer. He took her by the waist and carefully turned her around, taking the loose ends of her bra straps and hooking them together again.

He smoothed the sweater back down.

Only then, when those tempting bare inches of skin were safely covered, did he guide her back around.

Lazily, she raised her arms and rested them on his shoulders. "Oh, my." She let out a long, sweet sigh. "I think the chicken's burning."

He gritted his teeth to keep from taking her kiss-swollen mouth again. "Better see to it."

"Yes." She looked adorably regretful. "I suppose I'd better."

He let go of her—yet another impossible task somehow accomplished—and she turned for the stove.

The wine was right there and his glass was empty. He needed more. A river of it, to wash the tempting taste of her from his mouth—to numb the reality of what he was here to do. He filled his glass and topped off hers, too.

*I could...just drop the whole thing with Caleb,* he found himself thinking as he stood a few feet behind her, sipping more wine, his gaze tracking the length of her. From her gleaming, thick brown hair that curled sweetly at her shoulders, down to her trim waist, and lower still, over the smooth swell of her hips, along the shape of her thighs outlined beneath the slim skirt, and lower, to the backs of her slim calves. She sent him a smile over her shoulder as she moved from the stove to the oven again. From there, she came closer and set to work finishing the salad.

He watched her hands, narrow and smooth, clear polish on her short-trimmed nails.

*I could just never make my move,* he thought. *Let it all go ahead as Caleb believes it will. Give it up. At this point, no one would even have to know what I had meant to do.*

But then what?

Try to make his dream of a life with Katie come true?

And if he tried for that—what? Tell her the truth about himself? That basic fact that he'd lied—a whopping lie—in the first place, could ruin it between them.

So if not the truth, then what?

To hold forever within himself the central lie of his very existence? Seeing Caleb and his wife and their son all the time, becoming, in a sense, a part of the family?

No.

It was impossible.

He had to remember his mother. Remember Ramona Lovett, who called herself Ramona Caldwell. Remember the life they'd had. Barely holding on too much of the time. He had to remember, all of it.

Like that night when he was twelve. The night

she'd locked herself in the bathroom. Remember breaking down the door to find her limp in the bathtub, her forearms slit, bleeding out on the white tiles of the bathroom floor.

He'd slipped in her blood as he plowed through the medicine cabinet looking for something to staunch the flow.

After that, the Child Protective Services people had come sniffing around, so they'd moved. Again.

And then, always, he would have to live with the night she died.

She'd come to find him in Bozeman when she learned she wouldn't make it, come and let him take care of her for those final months. Once or twice, in the last weeks, she'd remarked that it was strange—maybe even meant to be. That he'd ended up here, in Western Montana, when she'd never once so much as brought him here the whole time he was growing up.

"I thought I raised you to live anywhere *but* here. And look. Here you are. Must be fate. Oh, yeah. Must be fate. When I'm gone you'll get your chance to make it all right."

He would ask her what she was getting at. What did Montana have to do with anything? And she would turn her head away.

Until the last. Until the night she died in the hospital, where he'd taken her once she couldn't get along without round-the-clock care.

"I know I never told you, who he was…your father. Maybe I should have." Her skeletal hand, tubes running from the back of it, weakly clutched his fingers. "Caleb. That's his name. Caleb Douglas. Wife,

Adele. They had one son. All they *could* have. Riley. In Thunder Canyon.''

"Thunder Canyon. That's right here. In Montana.''

She'd swallowed, sucked in another breath that wheezed like she was dragging it in through a flattened straw. Even the oxygen didn't help her by then. Nothing helped. "Yes. Twenty miles from here. In Montana. Caleb...'' she'd whispered, her eyes closing on a final sigh. "Caleb...''

And with that name on her lips, she was gone.

"Justin? Are you in there?'' Katie laughed, a light, happy sound. A sound from another world, a world of possibilities he couldn't let himself explore. "You should see your face. A million miles away.''

He shook himself. "Sorry.''

"Nothing to apologize for.'' She handed him the big wooden salad bowl. "Put this on the table? We'll just eat right here, in the breakfast nook, if that's okay?'' She handed him the salad tongs.

"Sounds good.'' He carried the bowl and tongs to the table, then helped her set it for two.

A few minutes later, she took out the potatoes, spooned them into a bowl, and transferred the chicken to a serving platter.

They sat down to eat. He looked at the food, and wondered if he'd be able to get anything down, though the chicken was crispy-brown and the potatoes perfectly cooked. The salad was crisp and green.

No. It wasn't the food.

It was the wrongness of being here, of holding her, of touching her soft body, kissing her lips, of drinking her wine and letting her cook for him.

Yeah. It was all wrong, to steal these last perfect moments with her, when in the end he could do nothing but continue on the course he'd set two years ago, on the day of his mother's death. In the end, his choice wouldn't change. He would get his payback—for Ramona Lovett Caldwell's sake, above all.

And that meant he had no right to sit here with Katie, in her house, at her table, pretending that there was some hope for the two of them.

There wasn't.

There never could be.

Katie set down her fork with a bite of potato still on the end of it. Justin had been much too quiet for several minutes now—ever since that kiss, as a matter of fact, a kiss that had almost ended with the two of them rushing to the bedroom.

But he had stopped it.

And ever since then…

"Justin, what is it?" She forced a joking laugh. "The food can't be that bad."

He pushed his plate away. "It's not the food." He really didn't look right.

Alarm skittered through her. His face was set. Kind of…closed against her. Why? "Was it something I said?" She tried to make the question light and playful, but didn't fully succeed. There was an edge to her voice. She couldn't help it.

She had the most powerful feeling that something had gone wrong.

Something major.

Something she had a sinking feeling she wasn't going to be able to make right.

Which was crazy. What could have gone wrong in the space of a few minutes? Hardly anything had been said.

"Justin, was it that you kissed me? But no. I don't see how it could be that." She raised both hands, palms up. "Did I do something to upset you? I just don't get it. I don't underst—"

He grabbed her hand. "Listen." He stood, pulling her up with him.

"Justin, I don't—"

"No. Hear me out. It's nothing you did." His eyes gleamed at her with a strange, wild kind of light.

"But if you—"

"No." He squeezed her fingers. Hard. "Wait. Listen."

She pulled her hand free of his, dread moving through her, dragging at her body, like an awful gravity from within. "All right." She folded her hands in front of herself, twining them together to keep from reaching out for him. He wouldn't like it if she tried to touch him now, she knew it, knew it in a deep and undeniable way.

Oh, what was up with him? How could something so right suddenly veer off into something so strange and wrong? It made no sense. And he still wasn't talking, in spite of telling her twice to listen. How could she listen if he had nothing to say?

"Justin, you're acting so strangely. Is something wrong? I'd appreciate it if you'd just tell me what's bothering—"

He interrupted. ''Nothing.'' The single word was far too curt. Not to mention a whopping lie.

''But if you'd only—''

''Listen.'' He reached out as if he would grab her, then jerked his hand back as though he'd been burned.

''But I've *been* listening. You're not talking.''

''It's only…I couldn't stay away. I missed you. I missed you like hell.''

She would have smiled in relief and delight, if only he hadn't sounded so angry about it. She made another feeble attempt at lightness. ''And this is a problem?''

He stared at her for a long, sizzling moment. She had the sense that he was going to spin on his heel and slam out the door. Why?

The word screamed in her mind.

*Why, why, why?*

''I shouldn't have come here. It was wrong.''

This was making no sense. No sense at all. ''Wrong? I don't see how. I invited you here. I wanted to make our dinner. I wanted to…be with you. I'm so glad you came.''

He stepped back abruptly, knocking over his chair, catching it at the last minute, righting it—and then turning, backing away from her, toward the door to the foyer. ''I should never have come. I only…''

She waited for him to finish, to say something that made sense. When he didn't, she prodded, ''You only, what?''

''I couldn't stay away.'' He hung his dark head. He looked so lost. So alone.

Her yearning heart went out to him. But when she

took a step toward him, he put up both hands, palms out, to keep her at bay. "No," he said, and, "No," again.

She stepped back, to show him she wouldn't come closer.

Oh, what was happening here? "It doesn't make sense. You say you couldn't stay away, that you missed me so much." It was like a sharp knife, turning in her belly, in her heart, in the very center of her, to admit it. But it had to be said. "I just don't see it. The way you're acting now, well, what am I supposed to think but that I've had it all wrong, about you and me?"

"No," he said flatly, his mouth twisting. "No. You weren't wrong. Not about that. Never about that."

"Then what?"

"Listen." He said that word again and he reached for her—again. Every atom in her body cried out to move toward him. But she made herself stay right where she was.

And, as before, his hands dropped to his sides. "I came here to tell you something." His voice was infinitely weary. "To tell you, and leave. I thought I'd do it over dinner, in a restaurant, where I wouldn't be tempted to…" The words trailed off. They both knew what he meant.

Tempted to kiss her.

Tempted to hold her.

Tempted to make sweet, passionate love with her.

They stared at each other across a short distance that felt like a million miles.

Finally, she made herself speak. "Do you still plan to say it, whatever it is?"

There was a slight hesitation, but then he nodded. "Yeah. I do."

She felt weary, too, now. Weary and sick at heart. Still, she straightened her spine and lifted her chin. "Then I guess you'd better say it, don't you think?"

He drew in a long breath and let it out hard. And, at last, he came out with it. "You're going to hate me, soon enough. But when you do, remember. None of it was about you. You shouldn't have been involved. It was one rotten step too far, what I did with you. A gross error in judgment on my part. You are exactly the woman a man like me never finds."

"But then I don't see why—"

"It's simple. I'm not who you think I am."

Her legs felt achy and rubbery. And her heart was a big lump of lead in her chest. She felt for the chair behind her. Slowly, with great care, she lowered herself into it. "I don't understand you. *What* wasn't about me? And if you're not who I think you are, well, who are you, then?"

There was a long, ugly silence. Finally, he muttered, "I can't say any more. Goodbye, Katie."

And that was it.

That was all.

Without another word, he turned and went out through the door to the foyer. She didn't follow him. She knew, in an awful, final kind of way that there was no point. A moment or two later, she heard the front door open—and close.

## Chapter Twelve

He had said she would hate him.

But she didn't.

She felt numb, as if she were floating, as if none of this was real.

The meal still waited, his plate untouched, hers almost the same, right there beside her on the table. She probably ought to go ahead and eat.

Through the numbness, she felt a touch of nausea.

No. No food. Not now.

She rose, very slowly, her legs wobbly and uncertain. Once she was on her feet, she leaned on the table for a moment or two, getting her bearings.

When she felt more certain her legs would hold her up, she calmly cleared the table and put the food away. She rinsed the dishes and put them in the dishwasher, washed the frying pan and hung it back on the overhead rack.

Once everything was cleaned up, all evidence of the meal they should have shared out of sight, once the sink was empty and the counters wiped down, she went through the door to the foyer, the same way he had gone. There, she locked the front door.

That taken care of, she turned for the stairs. As she climbed, she felt like someone very old and stiff, doggedly dragging herself up to bed. She held on to the polished railing, taking one careful step at a time.

What had happened, the things he'd said to her— none of it made any sense.

She only knew that it was over between them. Over before it had even really gotten started.

Beneath the ugly numbness, she knew she was going to have to get over him, get over a man who'd managed to fill up her world, to change everything, in the space of six days.

She hoped the numbness lasted awhile, bleakly aware that when it faded, she would have to deal with the pain of losing him, have to somehow learn to mend her shattered heart.

At eleven-thirty the next morning, Addy showed up at her door. "I came into town to pick up a few things and I thought we might go out and grab a bite of…" She peered at Katie closer. "Darling, what's happened? What's the matter with you?"

Squinting against the bright morning sun, Katie put her hand up to her tangled hair. "I…" She looked down at the pajamas she was still wearing. "I…well, I slept a little late."

Addy wasn't buying. She stepped over the threshold and closed the door firmly behind her. Quickly, she slipped out of her coat and hung it on the rack, then turned to face Katie again. "Something bad has happened. I can see it in your eyes." She grabbed Katie's hand and towed her into the living room, where she sat on the sofa and pulled Katie down beside her. "Now…" She seemed unsure of how to continue. "Oh, my dear. Please. Tell me what's happened."

Katie hadn't the faintest idea how to answer. She looked at the woman who'd been the mother she'd needed so much, the woman who'd come for her when she had no one else, the woman who'd been there, ever since, whenever Katie needed a listening ear or loving arms to hold her.

Katie realized she needed that now—Addy's loving arms around her. "Oh, Addy…"

Addy reached for her with a worried cry. "Now, now. Oh, honey."

Katie sagged into Addy's embrace, breathing in the faint scent of Addy's subtle perfume, feeling at least a little less numb.

Which maybe, on second thought, wasn't such a great thing. Something loosened in her chest. Without the numbness to keep them down, she felt the sudden tears rising. "Oh, Addy…"

"It's okay. It will be okay."

It wouldn't, and Katie knew it. Not for a long time. And that seemed so awful, so infinitely sad, that the tears rose high enough to burn her throat, to fill her eyes with scalding wetness. "Oh, I don't think so…oh, Addy, it won't. Not for a long time."

Her shoulders started shaking as the sobs took over, deep, wrenching ones. The tears dribbled down her cheeks and kept on coming, a river of them. Addy held her, not caring the least that Katie was soaking the front of her angora sweater. She whispered comforting words as Katie sobbed for the love—for the future with Justin—that was never going to be.

Finally, Katie spoke against Addy's warm, willing shoulder, the words fractured, broken—just like her heart. "It was…oh, Addy, I don't know how it happened, that I ended up caring so much. It shouldn't hurt like this, should it? It was only a few short days."

Addy stroked her hair. "Now, now…"

With another shuddering sob, Katie pulled free so she could meet Addy's eyes. "I—I think I love him," she said in terrified wonder. In complete disbelief. "But that can't be, can it? Not after so short a time, not after what happened last night—"

Addy asked the pertinent question. "Who, darling? Who do you love?"

Katie bit her lip. Suddenly she remembered: Caleb's ski resort project. It was so important to him. And this…what had happened, well, this was strictly personal. Between her and Justin. It had nothing to do with Caleb's business. But somehow, at that moment, she feared…

If Caleb found out how deeply Justin had wounded her, how she'd sobbed out her hurt and bewilderment in Addy's arms, he might confront Justin. He might even decide he couldn't allow Justin to be involved in his project.

She hadn't any idea what would happen then—maybe nothing. Or maybe Justin would back out and everything would have to be put on hold.

She didn't want that.

This wasn't about that.

"Addy, you have to promise me that you won't say a word to Caleb. I don't want him upset over this."

"Honey. Say a word about what?"

"You just have to promise me."

Addy's mouth pinched up tight. "It's that Justin Caldwell, isn't it?" When Katie only stared at her, she asked, outraged, "Well, who else could it be?"

Katie looked away.

Addy didn't allow that. "Look at me." Reluctantly, Katie did. Addy said, "It *is* Caldwell, isn't it?"

Katie only shut her eyes and wilted into Addy's arms again.

Addy held on tight. "There, there. Whatever he's done, I can see you're better off without him. You know that, don't you?"

The really awful, hopeless thing was that she didn't know it. She *still* didn't know it—oh, maybe in her head, she did. But not in her shattered heart, where it mattered. Even after he'd made it perfectly clear that she'd better learn to live without him, that he wouldn't be back, her hungry heart refused to believe it.

Somehow, though, she made herself nod against

Addy's shoulder. "Yes. I'm better off. I really am."
She pulled free of Addy's hold again and took the
tissue Addy handed her. She dried her tears and blew
her nose and drew herself up straight. "He broke it
off last night."

"You grew close in the museum?"

"Oh, Addy. It was a beautiful time. I felt as if I
knew him so well. It's so hard to explain. I felt this
powerful connection to him. I was so sure I'd found
the right guy."

"And then, out of nowhere last night, he told you
he wouldn't be seeing you anymore?"

"That's right."

"But why?"

It was the million-dollar question and Katie still
had no answer to it. "He didn't explain."

Addy grunted in pure disgust. "Some other
woman, no doubt."

"No. I really don't think so."

"Then what?"

"He just said it was over."

"But it makes no sense."

"That's what I've been thinking—*all* I've been
thinking. I've been trying to accept the fact that I'll
probably never know why he broke it off. I don't feel
very accepting, though. I really don't." She forced a
wobbly smile. "But, Addy. You're right. I'll be okay.
Eventually. I know I will."

Addy gave her a game grin. "That's the spirit."
Her grin became an angry frown. "And as for that
Caldwell fellow—"

Katie interrupted. "No. Listen. What happened was

strictly personal, between him and me. I shouldn't even have told you."

"Of course you should have," Addy huffed. "What affects you affects the people who love you. Never forget that." Addy sighed and took Katie's hand again, enclosing it between the two of hers. "Sometimes, when you're suffering terribly, it's hard to keep from cutting yourself off from the people who matter. Promise me you won't do that now."

There was something in Addy's voice, in her eyes. Something sad. And heavy with regret. Katie had to ask. "Have you done that? Cut yourself off from the ones who love you? Is that what you're saying?"

Addy patted her hand. "Am I so obvious?"

"Oh, no. Not at all. But I know you and love you. How you feel doesn't have to be obvious, for me to pick up on it—and it did seem to me as if you were talking about yourself just now."

There was a moment of silence. Then Addy admitted, "Well, yes. Maybe I was. I…well, I had a tough time when Riley was born. I almost didn't make it. And then they told me there would be no more children. I came from a big family and I always wanted, oh, ten or twelve or so of my own. I was cut to the heart by the news. I couldn't eat. Couldn't…love my husband. Or my new baby. The doctors said it was a serious case of postpartum depression."

"But…?"

"I don't know. I think maybe it was the death of my most cherished dream. To have a big family, to someday be surrounded by an adorable crowd of happy grandchildren. It hurt so much to lose that dream, I lost sight of all the wonderful things I *did* have. It was a terrible time. I almost drove Caleb away.''

''Impossible. He loves you so much.''

''I know. But he's a man who needs a lot of attention. You know him, full of life and energy. Always on to the next big plan. He needs a wife to help him live his dreams, a woman who's there, right beside him, while he makes those dreams come true. After Riley was born, I was like a shadow of myself, for much too long. And a man like Caleb can't live with a shadow for a wife. And certainly it wasn't any good for Riley, either. He was an innocent baby, then, a baby who needed his mother's love.''

''But you worked through it.''

''Yes. Barely. I should have reached out. But instead, I disengaged from the two people who needed me the most.'' Addy smoothed a wild strand of Katie's uncombed hair, guiding it back behind her ear. ''Don't make the same mistake yourself. Please.''

''I won't,'' Katie promised. ''But I do need a little time, you know? Addy, I really cared for him. It was sudden, yes. But somehow, being sudden and short-lived doesn't make it any less powerful.''

''I understand. I truly do. Just don't hold it all in. Just remember that we're here, Caleb and Riley and I, any time you need us.''

Addy stayed for lunch. As the two of them fixed sandwiches and heated up some soup, Addy asked more questions. She pressed for specifics about Justin, about what had gone wrong.

But Katie only shook her head. "It's over, that's all. All the little details don't matter." *Except to me.*

She couldn't get Addy to promise not to say anything about Justin to Caleb. "Business is business," Addy said. "But Caleb certainly has a right to know the kind of man he's dealing with."

Katie tried to argue that Addy didn't really know what kind of man Justin was. "You've just been complaining that I haven't told you anything. Remember that. I haven't. I didn't say anything against Justin, and I won't. All you know is there was…something. And now it's over."

"I know that he hurt you, and that's enough for me. Unless you're ready to tell me a little more about what happened?"

It was too much. "Let's just let it go for now. Please."

Addy looked slightly put out, but she did drop the subject. They ate lunch and Addy hung around for an extra cup of hot tea and then said she had to get back to the ranch. "Come for dinner tonight. Let us cheer you up."

"I can't. Not tonight. I need a few days. A little time to myself, to…lick my wounds, I guess. Maybe that's self-indulgent, but—"

"Oh, of course it's not," Addy cut in tartly. "You get through this however you need to. Just remember what I said before. Don't shut us out for *too* long."

"I won't. I promise you."

After Addy left, Katie wandered back upstairs to

her bedroom. She climbed into bed and closed her eyes. Sleep wouldn't come, so she simply lay there, wishing the numbness would return, feeling broken and much, much too sad.

Eventually, she dragged herself from bed, took a shower and forced herself to go out for a walk through Old Town. The snow lay in patches on the wet ground by then. It was hard to believe that it had been a deep, unbroken blanket of white just four days before. She waved at friends and neighbors she saw on the street and even stopped to chat with Emelda, who emerged from Super Savers Mart, the grocery store that had once been known as the Thunder Canyon Mercantile and had been owned and run by the Douglas family for generations.

"Will you look at this weather?" Emelda shifted her bag of groceries to one arm and stuck out the other in a gesture intended to include the wide, sunny sky and the melting patches of snow just beyond the covered sidewalk. "Amazing, isn't it? Snow past my eyeballs one day, dirty patches on the bare ground in no time at all—are you all right, dear? You do look a tad under the weather, and I know you didn't feel all that well last week." She leaned closer to Katie and kept on talking, saving Katie the discomfort of having to answer the question about how she was feeling. "One thing I did like about that nice, deep snow pack. Kept trespassers away from that erosion hole behind my back fence."

The hole in question was a caved-in section of tunnel from Caleb's played out mine, the Queen of Hearts. Riley had seen to boarding it over, but someone kept pushing the boards aside. Probably adventurous kids, Katie thought, kids wanting to holler down the hole and pitch rocks into the dark puddles of stagnant water at the bottom. Emelda worried constantly that someone was going to fall in. She'd called the Thunder Canyon police department more than once to report that she'd spotted trespassers around the hole.

"Those boards were moved again this morning," Emelda reported with a fretful cluck of her tongue. "I hope you'll speak to Riley about it. I worry, I do."

What else could she say? "I'll call Riley today."

"Thank you, dear. It's just that it's so dangerous."

Katie made a few more reassuring noises and then, at last, Emelda toddled off, headed up Pine, toward her tidy little house at the west end of State Street.

Katie walked on, trying to remember to smile and wave when folks said hi, though her mind kept tracking back to last night, to the way Justin had kissed her, so hungrily, as if he would never let her go, the way he had unhooked her bra and cupped her breasts, putting his hot mouth to them, the way his hands had stroked her, the way he'd gathered up her skirt, as if he had to touch her all over or die.

And then, not twenty minutes later, for no reason she could see, he was saying goodbye forever and walking out the door.

*None of it was about you. You shouldn't have been involved.* What did that *mean?*

*You are exactly the woman a man like me never finds....*

If she was so special, then *why* had he left her?

*I'm not who you think I am....*

It made no sense. None of it.

It made no sense and it hurt.

A lot.

When she got home, she resisted the temptation to put on her pj's again and climb back in bed. She went to the kitchen, thinking she'd try focusing on what to have for dinner.

Easily handled. She had plenty of leftovers.

But when she pulled open the refrigerator door and looked at the covered dish full of chicken, at the plastic containers with the salad and potatoes inside, the bittersweet memory of last night overwhelmed her.

She saw him at the sink, scrubbing the potatoes; at the counter, handing her the slotted spoon. She could almost hear their voices, talking of everyday things, could see his smile and the warmth and admiration in his eyes.

Swiftly, before she could feel guilty for wasting good food, she took out the covered dish and the plastic containers and emptied them into the trash.

There. Now didn't that help a lot?

Hardly. Still, she would never eat that food and she was glad it was gone.

And there was still Riley. She'd promised Emelda she'd give him a call, though she didn't really feel like talking to anyone right at that moment. Reluctantly, she dialed his number. His machine picked up and relief flowed through her. She left a quick message about the problem at the erosion hole and hung up. There. She'd kept her word to Emelda and she hadn't had to listen to Riley's dear deep voice, hadn't been faced with the possibility he might pick up on her misery and want to know if something was bothering her.

She went upstairs early and lay in bed forever, pretending to sleep.

Sunday, Addy called after church. "We missed you at the service."

"I just felt like staying home today."

"Honey, now remember what we talked about. You can't let yourself—"

"Addy. It's only been two days."

"I know, I know. I guess I just, well, I want to make things all better."

Katie suppressed a sigh. "You can't. Not right now. I'm okay. Really." As okay as could be expected, anyway, given the circumstances.

"You're right. Of course you're right. I couldn't possibly talk you into coming on out to the ranch for dinner, now could I?"

"Next Friday. How's that?"

"And our usual lunch on Thursday."

"Of course."

"You call me. I mean it. If you need anything."

"Oh, Addy. You make it sound as if I've got some terrible disease."

"Sorry. Remember. I'm here."

Katie almost chuckled. "As if I could forget."

Addy clucked over her and urged her to take care of herself and finally said goodbye.

Katie spent a peaceful day, reading, taking a long

walk, watching television in the evening. She told herself she was feeling better, and she was.

Maybe. In a way.

Monday she went to work at nine, as usual.

Lindy was waiting for her, an avid gleam in her eyes. "Katie. Wow. That Justin Caldwell…total hunk. So did you have a great time Friday night, or what?"

It hurt—that cruel knife, twisting—just to hear his name. "Yes," she said flatly. "Great." And it had been, until the end. "And don't you have work to do?"

Lindy stepped back. "Well, excuse me for breathing."

Katie knew she'd skirted the borderline of rudeness, but somehow, right then, she didn't have it in her to smooth things over. She turned for her workstation in the center of the room.

The whole day, she did her very best to keep her mind on task. Neither Lindy nor Emelda asked if there was anything wrong with her. But she caught both of them looking at her, sideways looks of confusion and concern.

That night, at home, she tried to read, but it was no good. She didn't have the concentration for it, not right then. So she turned on the television and stared at the changing images, hardly aware of what she was watching.

Her mind kept circling back to the central question, kept worrying at it, trying to make sense of it….

Not for another woman. She would have bet every cent she had on that. And not for her money, either.

If it had been about her money, he'd still be there, he wouldn't have left. He'd be busy sweeping her off her feet, getting ready to propose marriage for real, paving the way at a chance for a big payoff when it came time for a divorce.

And if not for another woman, or for the money, then *why?*

She simply could not understand.

Why?

## Chapter Thirteen

The meeting of the Thunder Canyon Ski Resort Investor Group was scheduled for ten on Tuesday morning, in the conference room at the back of the project offices on Main Street.

It was to be a strictly routine proceeding. As project manager, Caleb would sit at the head of the table and run the meeting, explaining the current status of the project to any investors who happened to show up. He would list the contractors who would supervise construction and assure everyone that the financing was in order and building would be ready to begin in May, right after the gala groundbreaking ceremonies.

Justin arrived at fifteen before the hour—which was fifteen minutes too early. When it came to dropping bombs, it was always advisable not to hang around the water cooler making casual chitchat beforehand.

The wrong subject might come up. He'd have to evade or lie outright and that could lead to questions he didn't want to answer—at least not before the crucial moment.

No. Better to be right on time, go straight to the conference room, ready to blow them all—Caleb most especially—out of their fat leather chairs.

In the lot behind the town hall, Justin parked and turned off the engine and sat behind the wheel, ready to dig into his briefcase and look busy if anyone noticed him just sitting there.

As he waited, he tried to keep his thoughts where they belonged: on the final stroke ahead. On his payback, at last.

Instead, his mind kept wandering to the one subject he had sworn to himself he would avoid.

Katie.

He stared out the windshield and saw nothing but her face: those wide amber eyes, that soft mouth, the shining brown hair.

She'd be at the library now, wouldn't she? Standing behind that central counter, ready to help any reader who needed to know where to find a certain book. She'd be—

A tapping sound on the driver's door window cut into his self-indulgent reverie. He turned his head.

Caleb. Damn it.

The older man swept off his big white Stetson and signaled with a jerk of his head.

No way to fake being busy now. Justin grabbed his briefcase and got out of the SUV.

"We've got a minute or two before the meeting,"

Caleb said, without any of the back-slapping how-you-been-and-good-to-see-you routine that was his usual style. "I want a word with you."

"What's up?" Alarm bells jangling along every nerve, Justin tried to keep it casual, despite the cold look on Caleb's tanned, creased face.

But even if the silver-haired wheeler-dealer had somehow found out what was up, there wasn't a thing he could do about it now. It was, in the truest sense, a done deal. Justin had the needed proxies in his briefcase and he *would* make his move.

Caleb didn't answer his question. "Let's go inside, to my office."

They went in the back way, Caleb ushering Justin ahead. The door to Caleb's private office stood open and Justin led the way in.

"Have a seat." Caleb shut the door.

Justin stayed on his feet. "Is there a problem?"

Caleb sent the white Stetson flying. It landed on a sofa in the small sitting area. He strode around Justin and pulled out the studded leather chair behind his wide inlaid desk. But he didn't sit down. He moved in front of the chair, pressed his knuckles to the desktop and loomed toward Justin. "What's this I hear about you breaking my little girl's heart?"

Katie.

Damn it to hell. He should have known. "She... went to you?"

Caleb snorted. It was not a friendly sound. "Hell, no. Adele got it out of her. But it doesn't make a damn how I know. The point is, whatever you thought you were up to with her, you've messed her over and I want to know why."

Justin stared at the stranger who had fathered him. This was exactly the way it was supposed to go.

So why didn't he feel the least bit triumphant? Why didn't he feel righteous and eager to deal the final blow instead of fed up with this whole thing, fed up and sick at heart, an ashy taste in his mouth?

"I asked you a question." Caleb craned farther across the big desk.

The words came to Justin, the ones he'd once imagined himself saying. He went ahead and spoke them. He had nothing else to say. "It's interesting how concerned you are for the tender feelings of your wife's goddaughter, when you never spared a thought for the woman who did nothing wrong but to love you—and bear your son."

Caleb blinked. "Never spared a thought. For Addy? I don't know what the hell you're blathering about."

"You'll understand everything. I promise you. Soon enough."

"I don't know what you think is going on here. But I'll tell you this. You hurt my Katie—for no damn reason that anyone can see. And I'm not going to forget it."

Justin glanced at his Rolex. "Time for the meeting. I think we should go in."

Prior to the formal start of the meeting, the investors milled around, exchanging greetings, while Caleb's secretary bustled up and down the big table, carrying coffee to anyone who asked for it and bringing extra water glasses. A thick blue file imprinted with the ski resort logo of a downhill racer crouched and flying along a snowy slope waited at every seat.

Eventually, Caleb cleared his throat and suggested that everyone sit down. He settled into his seat at the head of the long table and glanced around at the investors. "Well. We have a pretty nice turnout." There were a few empty seats, including the ones that should have been filled by Verlin Parks and Josh Levitt. Verlin and Josh had thirteen and fifteen percent of the project, respectively. With Justin's twenty-six percent, that made a total of fifty-four. Three percent more than he needed, as a matter of fact. Caleb added, "Let's begin."

Up and down the table there were murmurs of agreement.

And so they began.

Caleb led them through the file. He was pleased—though he sent a hard look Justin's way as he said it—to announce that the project was a definite go. The financing was taken care of, and the contractors lined up. Justin sat and pretended to listen. He was only waiting for the proper moment.

Waiting and wishing that he even gave a damn anymore. Longing to get up and walk out and let Caleb have his damn project.

But he didn't get up. He would do what he'd come to do. He would make Caleb Douglas pay in the way that mattered most to him: Justin would take away control.

And *wishing* was an activity for fools, anyway.

He kept having to remind himself of that.

Ever since he'd met a certain amber-eyed brunette who'd made him start *wishing* for what he was never going to have.

Finally, it was time. Caleb asked, "Well, gentlemen. Is there any other business we need to discuss?"

And Justin said, "Yes, as a matter of fact, there is. There's the question of who's going to manage the project."

The room went dead silent—until Caleb boomed out, "What the hell are you talking about? I'm project manager. We're all in agreement on that. I'm listed as manager on the limited partnership contract that everyone here has signed."

There were murmurs and nods down the table.

Justin spoke again. "I have another man in mind. He's got the experience. Much more so than you, Caleb."

Beneath his deep tan, a hot flush rushed up the older man's neck. "I *have* the experience. And I have everyone's support but yours." There were more nods and whispers of agreement. Caleb blustered on, "It's been a given from the first that this was my baby and I would be in charge. The financing was arranged with that understanding. If anyone tries to change horses in midstream, the money could fall through."

Justin didn't waver. "If the current financing becomes a problem, I'll see that we find another lender. It's not going to be a problem. As you just spent an hour telling us, the project is in excellent shape. And as to your holding majority support…" He reached in his briefcase and pulled out the two proxies. He tossed them down on the table. "Joshua Levitt and Verlin Parks are in support of any decision I make. Here are their proxies to prove it."

The flush had left Caleb's face. Now he looked a little green. Justin could see in his eyes that until that moment, he hadn't guessed that Verlin and Josh were longtime business associates of Justin's—or that Justin had sent them in ahead to buy in for specific amounts. Caleb spoke low and furiously. "All right, Caldwell. What the hell is going on?"

Justin only shrugged. "As I said, Verlin and Josh have given me their proxies. I now speak for them. Look the proxies over. Please. You'll see they're in order. Between Parks, Levitt and me, we hold fifty-four percent. More than enough to choose a new project manager—according to the terms of the partnership."

Again, the room was pin-drop silent.

Then Darrell Smart spoke up. "Let's have a look." Darrell was one of Caleb's good buddies, and legal counsel for the project. Justin shoved the proxies toward the lawyer. Smart picked them up and studied them in a silence so total, the crackling of the papers as he handled them sounded loud as gunshots.

Finally, the attorney glanced over the top of his reading glasses at Caleb. "Sorry. Looks in order to me."

Caleb barely seemed to hear him. He was too busy glaring at Justin. Justin could read what he was thinking as if the older man had spoken aloud. *Why are you doing this? What the hell does it prove?*

Justin dealt the telling blow. "All right, then. I

move that we put in my man as manager. Since I hold control of fifty-four percent of this partnership, what I move, goes." He granted Caleb a frosty smile. "And since these offices are part of the project, I'll expect you to turn them over. My man will be here next Monday, ready to get to work."

There was some discussion—heated, but pointless. In the end, everyone conceded that Justin had the power to bring in his own manager. Caleb was finished as project head.

Finally, after sending Justin lethal looks and offering regrets to the by-then silent Caleb for the dirty trick that had been played on him, the others filed out.

Caleb remained in his chair, his gray head lowered, as the others took their leave. His left arm lay lax on the tabletop, his thick gold wedding ring gleaming in the shaft of winter sunlight that slanted in the room's one tall, narrow window.

Finally, it was just the older man, slumped in his big chair, Justin, still seated in his, and the secretary.

"Alice, you can go now," Caleb said quietly, not bothering to glance up. The secretary, looking wide-eyed behind her thick glasses, rose. "Shut the door on the way out, will you?"

Alice did as she was told, pulling the door quietly closed as she left.

There was a long moment where Caleb simply sat there, head lowered as before, arm still outstretched on the table, wedding ring catching the light, giving back that eerie gleam.

Eventually, he rested his other arm beside the first, folded his beefy hands together and lifted his head. His green eyes had a lost look in them, one of shock and dazed confusion. He said one word. "Why?"

The question echoed in the silent room.

And Justin had his answer ready. "Because being the big dog, running everything in sight—that's what matters to you the most. I wanted to take away something you'd miss. And I have, haven't I?"

Caleb still wasn't satisfied. "Why?" he asked again. "Why would you want that? What the hell have I ever done to you?"

Justin reached in his briefcase again and brought out an envelope. From the envelope, he removed two snapshots. He pushed his chair back, rose to walk down the table and stood over the other man.

Shoving the ski resort file aside, he laid the pictures down, one beside the other, in front of Caleb. He pointed. "That's my mother, thirty-five years ago, before she met you."

Caleb stared down at the old, dog-eared snapshot. "Ramona…" It came out a bare husk of sound.

Relentless now, determined to finish this and get out, Justin pointed at the other picture. "That one was taken a month before she died. She came to me, returned to Montana at the end, so I could take care of her, when it was too late for anything else—too late for you to do anything to her that cancer wasn't going to do, anyway. She doesn't look much like the woman you knew, does she?"

Caleb raised his eyes then. He'd moved beyond dazed confusion. Now he looked like a man who'd seen a ghost—which, in a way, Justin supposed, he had. His face had a gray cast beneath the tan. "But…her last name was Lovett."

"That's right. But after you told her you wanted nothing more to do with her—or the baby you'd made with her—she left the state, just the way you wanted her to. She left Montana and she never returned until she knew she was dying. When she left, she took the name Caldwell. She went by that name for the rest of her life. She put it on my birth certificate. So that's who I am."

Caleb shut his eyes and slowly opened them. "You're…my son." He said it in a kind of horrified understanding. "My son…"

"By blood, yes. By blood only. You broke her, do you know that? She never could make a real life for herself, after what you did to her, after you threatened to do her serious damage if she ever came near you again, if she ever dared to let anyone know whose child she was carrying."

Caleb jerked back as if Justin had struck him. "No. You've got it—"

Justin cut the air with an arm, a brutal, final gesture. "I don't want to hear it."

"But you have to listen for a moment. You have to let me—"

"That's where you're wrong. I don't have to listen to you. Who are you to me, besides the man who destroyed the woman who gave me life, the woman who raised me the best she knew how?" He scooped up the two snapshots and turned for the door, stopping before he went out to deliver one last command.

"Clear out your office. My man will be in Monday morning, nine sharp."

## Chapter Fourteen

Katie's phone rang at nine Tuesday night. She picked up the remote extension and checked the display before she answered it: Addy.

"No, thanks. Not right now," she muttered, and let her machine get it. She settled back in her favorite chair, and heard the sound of Addy's voice coming from the kitchen, as she recorded her message.

Katie couldn't make out the words, but there was something in the tone, something agitated. Something not right.

With a sigh, she picked it up. "Addy? Are you okay?"

"Oh, thank God."

Whatever it was, it wasn't good. Grim images invaded Katie's mind: Riley, in an accident. Caleb having a heart attack. "What? What's the matter?"

"Darling, it's Caleb."

She felt a hollowness below her ribs. "Has he been hurt?"

"Not physically. No. It's nothing like that. He… Well, he's locked himself in his study. He's been in there since noon. Nine hours. He won't come out and he won't let anyone else in."

"But why?"

"Sweetheart, if I only knew. I called Riley over here a couple of hours ago, when I couldn't get Caleb to open the door myself. Riley's tried. Caleb wouldn't let him in, either. Honey, it's just not like him. He came home from that meeting and he walked right by me. He looked so awful. Not sick, exactly. But sick at heart. Kind of beaten down and gray in the face, his shoulders slumped and sagging. I asked him what was wrong, but he only shook his head and headed for his study."

"Addy, what meeting?"

"The one for the ski resort project."

"Something bad happened at the meeting?"

"Well, if it did, he's just not acting his usual self over it. You know how he is. When things don't go his way, he paces. He gets loud and he lays down the law. But he never locks himself in a room somewhere and refuses to come out. Plus, I'm sure he's drinking. The times he barked at me through the door to go away, he was slurring his words."

"Have Riley call someone who was at the meeting and ask them what went on there."

"Oh, honey. Yes. Good idea." Katie heard her

speaking to Riley. Then she came back on the line. "All right. Riley's taking care of that."

"I'll be over as soon as I can get there."

"Darling, would you? I'm so worried. And you know how he adores you. Maybe he'll open that door for you."

Addy greeted her at the front door, her face drawn, eyes grim with worry. She helped Katie out of her coat and hung it in the front closet of the huge two-story foyer as she blurted out what she knew. "Riley got through to Darrell Smart. At the meeting, Justin Caldwell took the job of project manager away from Caleb."

Katie's heart lurched. "Justin...but how?"

"Oh, it was something about proxies. And percentages of the partnership. Somehow, that Caldwell fellow got control over enough of the investors to be able to kick Caleb out. Caleb has until Monday to vacate the offices so the new man can take over."

Could this really be happening? Justin. Breaking her heart, then stealing Caleb's dream.

The question was there again, echoing through her mind. She said it out loud that time. "Why would he do such a thing?"

"I haven't the foggiest. But if that man were in this room right now, I'd go get Caleb's best hunting rifle and shoot him straight through his evil heart. What did Caleb ever do to him, that he would treat my husband so shabbily—and for that matter, what did *you* ever do to him?" Addy answered her own questions. "Nothing. Absolutely nothing, that's what.

And now Riley's in a fury over it. He's insisting he's going to Bozeman to confront Caldwell. Oh, I don't know where we're headed, I don't know what to do.''

Katie took the older woman by the upper arms, to steady her. ''Slow down. We're going to get to the bottom of this, I promise you.''

''Oh, Katie. I'm sorry to drag you into this, but I must admit, I'm so relieved you're here. I'm…well, I'm just a wreck.''

Katie pulled her close and hugged her hard, then she took her arms again and met her eyes. ''First, I'll talk to Riley, get him to slow down a little. And then we'll see if I can get Caleb to let me in.''

Katie found Riley in Caleb's den, off the study, pacing back and forth. He was hot under the collar and far from willing to slow down.

''Good. You're here,'' he said at the sight of her. ''Look after Mom, will you? I'm heading for Bozeman.''

Katie grabbed one of his big, tanned hands and wouldn't let go. ''Please. Let me try to talk to Caleb first. Let me see if I can find out what's really happened here.''

Riley's green eyes shone hard as emeralds. ''I know what's happened. That bastard worked you over, and now he's done this. If there's a reason he's decided to come after my family, I want to find out what it is.''

So, Katie thought glumly. Riley knew about her and Justin, too. She supposed she shouldn't be surprised. Adele had never agreed not to tell Caleb. And once Caleb knew, Riley was bound to hear. "We all want answers." She squeezed Riley's hand between both of hers. "I beg you. Give me a chance to get to the bottom of this first. Then, if you still think you have to, you can go deal with Justin."

Riley made a low, angry sound. "Face it. Dad's not letting you through that door."

"Just give me a chance. Please."

Riley swore low. "All right. But if he won't let you in, I'm out of here."

"Thank you."

"No reason to thank me. He's not letting you in."

She gave his hand one more reassuring squeeze and then relinquished it.

Riley gestured at the shut door to the study. "Go for it." He stood back and folded his muscular arms over his broad chest, his mouth set in a grim line.

Riley was probably right. If Caleb wouldn't open the door for his wife or his son, there was no reason to believe he'd let Katie in, either. But she had to try. She didn't like the look in Riley's eyes. If Riley took off after Justin now, who could say what might happen when the two met up. One of them—or both— could get hurt. She didn't want that. Not for Riley. And, God help her, not for Justin, either.

She marched over, raised her hand and rapped sharply on the door.

Nothing. Complete silence from the room beyond. She glanced back at Riley. He still had his arms folded over his chest—and an I-told-you-so look in his eyes. She tried the door: locked.

Riley muttered, "See, I told—"

Katie put up a hand to silence him and called to the man on the other side of the door. "Caleb. It's me, Katie. Won't you let me in, please?"

Dead silence from beyond the door. Riley uncrossed his arms. "That does it. I'm—"

"Wait." She pressed her ear to the door, heard heavy footsteps on the other side. She put up her hand again, for Riley to be still.

The footsteps stopped. Caleb spoke from right beyond the door. "Katie? That you?"

"Yes. Oh, yes. It's me."

"Katie, I don—" He didn't seem to know how to go on. And Adele had been right. It sounded as if he'd been drinking. His words came slow and slurred-sounding.

"Oh, Caleb. Won't you let me in?"

Another pause, then Caleb growled, "Riley still out there?"

She glanced at Riley again. He looked as if he wanted to break something, to pick up one of the bronze cowboy sculptures that decorated the den and hurl it at the wood-paneled wall. "Yes. He's here."

"Tell him to go 'way. Can't talk to 'im now. Only you, Katie. Jus' you, 'kay?"

Riley muttered more swear words. Katie only looked at him, pleading with her eyes.

With another low, furious oath, Riley strode from the room.

"Katie?" Caleb asked again.

"It's all right. Riley's left. Now, won't you please let me in?"

Almost before she finished asking the question, the door swung inward.

She gasped at the sight of the man on the other side. "Oh, Caleb..." His green eyes were droopy and bloodshot. His mouth hung lax. He looked a decade older than the last time she'd seen him. And the smell of too much Tennessee whisky came off him in waves.

He gave her the saddest, most hangdog sort of look, and then he turned and trudged to his wide burled walnut desk and around to the back of it. With a heavy grunt, he dropped into his studded buckskin swivel chair and stared down at the papers spread on the desktop in front of him. A telltale half-empty bottle of whisky stood uncapped at his elbow. "I been...busy. Thinkin'. Thinkin' and drinkin'..." He looked up, let out a low, rough bark of humorless laughter, and then leaned back in the chair. His chin drooped on his chest. He gazed mournfully at the scatter of papers in front of him. "How, I keep askin' mysel'...how did it all go so wrong...?" Behind him, a picture hung askew on the wood-paneled wall, revealing his private safe, the door to which stood open. All the blinds were drawn and the only light came from the lamp on Caleb's desk.

Katie hovered before him, a million dismayed questions spinning through her mind. She pressed her mouth shut and kept quiet. She knew, in the end, he would tell her what she needed to know. There was no other reason for him to have let her in here when he refused to open the door to Adele or to Riley.

He *wanted* to talk. And he'd chosen her to do his

talking to. It was only a matter of waiting and listening—and applying gentle pressure at the right moment.

Gingerly, she lowered herself to one of the two carved, leather-seated guest chairs that faced the big desk. Once she was in the chair, she realized she'd been holding her breath. She let it out with great care.

Caleb shook his head. "Katie, Katie, Katie. Where the hell did it all go so wrong?" He raised his hanging head enough that she could look into those bleary eyes.

"Tell me," she said softly. "Just tell me. Everything. And then we can talk about what to do next."

He kept shaking his head. "Bad idea. To tell you. Yeah. Pro'ly a bad idea…"

"Just tell me. We can't work this out until you do."

"Hell. I don't know…"

"Oh, yes, you do. You know. It's time to talk about it—whatever it is."

"Maybe."

"Uh-uh. No maybes. It's time. You know it is."

He regarded her woozily. She looked back at him, waiting.

At last, haltingly, he began to speak. "I was…a true husban'. I swear it to you. Never looked at another woman…"

Suddenly she was recalling what Addy had told her a few days before and prompted gently, "But then Riley was born…"

He grunted. "Tha's right. Riley. Af'er Riley was born, they tol' Adele she couldn't have any more chil'ren. It broke her heart. Lo's o' kids. She always wanted that. For the longes' time, she was…like a stranger in our house…in our bed. She jus' ignored me. An' Riley, too. Poor little fella. He was cryin' all the time. I couldn'…take it. It got so I, well, I jus' needed someone.''

He said he'd met Ramona one night when he went out to a roadhouse to get his mind off his vacant-eyed wife and their poor, screaming baby. ''Ramona was a waitress. A tall, black-haired beauty.'' He heaved a heavy sigh. ''Ramona. Damn my soul. Ramona.''

For over an hour, his voice low and whisky-rough, the words sometimes slurring together, he told her the sad story of his own folly and betrayal. When the tale was told, Katie sat silent, hardly able to believe what she'd just heard.

Justin was Caleb's son. His *son.*

Suddenly, everything was making sense. A hideous, awful, ugly kind of sense, but sense nonetheless.

Caleb threw out a hand—missing the whisky bottle by an inch. In a sweeping, unsteady gesture, he indicated the papers scattered on his desk. ''I's all here. Righ' here…you jus' see for yourself.''

Katie stood and bent over the desk.

''See. Look here.'' He waved a snapshot. ''Ramona an' me.'' He dropped the picture and picked up what looked like a letter. ''Her love letters. She wro'e me a hundred of 'em. Sen' 'em here, to the house. Addy never knew. She wasn' up for checkin' the mail. She jus' stayed in our room, then. Alone. I hardly saw her. Ramona wro'e me, love letters first.

And then there were the ones that came later, the ones with the threats.'' He scanned the desk and snatched up a small scrap of paper. ''An' this. The check I gave 'er. Jus' like I tol' you, cancelled. See?''

Katie took it from his fingers. ''Yes. I see.'' It came to her, right then, as she stared at all those zeroes. She knew what she had to do.

''I—I did care for her, for Ramona,'' Caleb muttered. ''But...she wasn' Addy. Addy is...my love, my life. Never should have started up with Ramona. I know it, I do. And then, well, after Ramona disappeared, Addy got better. The years went by an'...I started thinkin' it was maybe for the bes', jus' to let it be, not go stirrin' up ol' trouble.''

A large yellow envelope lay at the edge of the desk. Katie took it and dropped the cancelled check into it. Then she gathered up the letters and the photographs and put them in the envelope, too.

''What d'you think you're doin'?'' Caleb demanded.

She hooked the envelope's metal clasp. ''I'm taking these to Justin.''

He regarded her blearily. ''Wha' for?''

''Because he doesn't know the whole truth, and it's time he did.''

Caleb rubbed his eyes. ''Hell. What good's that gonna do now?'' He was shaking his head again. ''No point. Too late.''

''Caleb,'' she said softly. ''It's never too late to do the right thing.'' Turning, she set the envelope on her chair, then she went around the desk and put her hand on Caleb's sagging shoulder.

He looked up at her, a lost look. "I...don' know what to do."

She squeezed his shoulder. "First, and foremost, you have to remember that Adele loves you. And, though I know you've had your rough patches, Riley loves you, too."

"They'll hate me. After this."

"No," she said firmly. "They love you. I'm not saying it will be easy, getting past this. You've done wrong. Very wrong. Not only because you betrayed your wife, but also because of the way you handled it when Ramona told you she was having your baby. But now you've got to clean up the mess you made, as best you can. You've got to tell Adele everything. You've got to take the first steps toward making things right."

"Oh, no. I can't." His head hung down again.

"Look at me," she commanded. Slowly, he raised his bloodshot eyes. "Caleb, you can't let this break you, can't let the bad things you did once destroy your family now."

"But I—"

"No buts. It's the only way."

He tried to bluster. "I didn' let you in here so you could tell me what to do."

"Yes, you did. That's exactly why you let me in here."

He let out a hard breath that reeked of too much whisky. "Oh, no..."

"Oh, yes. You need to do the right thing and you know it. You let me in here so I could help you to do it." She touched his silver hair, pressed his shoulder again. "I'm going to go get Addy now. And you're going to tell her. Everything."

He said nothing and she figured that was acceptance enough. She turned for the door.

"Katie?"

She glanced back at his hangdog face, his haunted eyes. "You're a good girl, my bes' girl."

"I love you, too. Put the cap on that bottle. I'll be right back."

A half an hour later, Riley walked her to her Suburban. She had the envelope in hand, Justin's home address and phone number scrawled across the front of it.

"Thanks," Riley said, and gave her a hug.

"Any time." She hugged him back, good and hard.

When he pulled away, he looked doubtful. "You sure you don't want me to go with you, to see Caldwell?"

"Nope. I'll be fine."

"Damn." He raked a hand back through his dark hair. "What a mess, huh? And I've got a half brother..."

"Yes. You do."

"That'll be something to get used to—after I get through telling Dad just what I think of him."

She suggested gently, "Wait 'til he's sober. For tonight, Addy's going to need your strong shoulder to lean on once she's through dealing with Caleb."

Riley swore. "At least what Caldwell did to Dad is more understandable now. If I were in his position, I might have done a lot worse." He scowled. "But there's still no excuse for what he did to you. I could bust his face in for that.''

She put her hand on his arm. "No need to go hitting anyone. I can handle this. You watch me.''

He almost grinned. "You know, I believe that you can.'' He chucked her under the chin. "You're a tough little tenderfoot.''

"That's me. Tough as they come.''

He grew more serious. "When will you go?''

She looked up into his face and for the first time, she saw the resemblance to Justin. In the shape of his brow and the strong, aggressively masculine jut of his jaw. So strange. Why hadn't she noticed before?

Riley was frowning. "Katie. You okay?''

She drew herself up. "I'm fine. And I'm going to go see Justin right now. It'll be near midnight when I get there. I'm figuring that's late enough on a weeknight he'll probably be at his house.'' Plus, if she went right away, there was less of a chance she'd lose her nerve.

Riley gave her a sideways look. "You sure about this?''

"Riley, he needs to know and, given the circumstances, I think I'm the best one to tell him.''

Justin was sitting in his study at the front of the house when the doorbell rang.

His laptop waited, open and ignored, on the desk before him. His mind was far away from the spreadsheet on the screen, stuck on a brown-haired woman and a silver-haired man and why he didn't feel the sense of triumph and vindication he'd always expected to feel after finally making his move.

The doorbell chimed and Justin ignored it.

He wasn't expecting anyone; he didn't want to see anyone—and anybody who came ringing his bell at midnight could damn well go away and come back at a decent hour.

But then, a minute later, the doorbell rang again. "Get lost," he muttered, and stared blindly at the computer screen in which he had no interest at all.

But then it rang a third time.

That did it. He swore, low and crudely, and pushed himself to his feet. Whoever was out there was going to get an earful.

He strode, fast, through the door to his study and across the hardwood floor of the entry hall. When he got to the door, he flung it wide.

"Hello, Justin."

The breath fled his lungs. He felt as if an iron hand had just punched him a good one square in the solar plexus. He blinked and stepped back. "Katie."

"May I come in?"

"What—?"

She cut him off, sweetly but firmly. "I said, may I come in?"

He fell back another step. He just wasn't getting this. What reason could she possibly have to seek him out now?

It made no sense. Katie, here. At his door.

And still, though it gained him nothing but more pain, he couldn't help drinking in the sight of her, of her shining hair and angel's face, of the grim set to her soft mouth and the strange, determined gleam in those beautiful brown eyes. The scent of her taunted him—warm and temptingly sweet.

*Katie.* All his senses seemed to call out her name.

"I'll take that as a yes." She stepped over the threshold. She had a big envelope in one hand. She waved it at him. "I have a few things I need to say to you. Is there somewhere we can talk?"

Quelling the urge to sputter out more exclamations of disbelief that she was standing right there, in front of him, he muttered, "Yeah. All right."

She slipped out of her coat, switching the envelope from hand to hand as she shrugged free of the sleeves.

"Here." He reached for it.

But she held on. "No. I'll keep it. This shouldn't take long."

The more he looked at her, the more certain he was that he didn't like the strange gleam in her eyes.

But why should he like it? No way she'd come here to tell him she loved him and couldn't live without him.

Any chance he'd had for that, he'd blown Friday night—and doubly, at the meeting fourteen hours before. Which meant it was going to be something he didn't want to hear.

Might as well get it over with. "Suit yourself." He turned on his heel. "This way."

He led her to the great room at the back of the house, where the ceiling soared up two stories high and two walls of windows looked out on the night. She perched on a chair in one of the sitting areas and folded her coat in her lap. He hovered a few feet from her.

"Please," she said. "Sit down."

He wanted to refuse, felt he'd be better off to stay on his feet. But she looked up at him, mouth set, amber eyes afire with a steely sort of purpose. He gave in and dropped into the chair across from her.

She bit her lip. "I…hardly know where to begin."

He said nothing. It was her damn show, after all.

She sat up straighter and cleared her throat. "Okay. To start, I know about what you did to Caleb this— or rather yesterday—morning. I also know why, at last. I know that you're his son, that he had an affair with your mother when Addy suffered a serious bout of depression after Riley was born. Caleb couldn't take it, watching Addy suffer—her continued rejection of him. He met your mother and they had an affair."

Impatience curled through Justin, coiling like a spring. He wanted her out of there. Every moment in her presence brought it more clearly home to him that he had lost her.

Hell, lost her? He'd never *had* her.

And he never would.

He demanded, "Is there some reason you imagined I needed—much less, *wanted*—to hear all this?"

Her sweet mouth got a pinched look about it. "Be a little patient. Please. I'm getting to the part you need to know."

"Speed it up."

She outright glared at him. "Fine," she said. "It went like this. Caleb and your mother had an affair.

When your mother got pregnant, Caleb told her he did care for her, but he still loved Adele. He wouldn't marry your mother, but he offered to give her a half million dollars. For you.''

He couldn't stay in his seat. He shot to a standing position. ''That's ridiculous. It never happened.''

A hot flush flowed up her neck and over her soft cheeks. ''Will you let me finish?''

He turned from her, stared at his own shadowed reflection in the dark window opposite where she sat. ''Make it fast.''

She picked up the pace, each word emerging clipped and cold. ''Caleb offered your mother five hundred thousand dollars if she'd give you up, if she'd give you to him—so he and Adele could raise you. Somehow, he hoped to make Adele understand and accept you into their family. It might even have worked. Addy wanted more children so badly.''

He whirled on her. ''So what? It doesn't matter. My mother turned him down and then he started threatening her. She had to run away.''

''No. She didn't turn him down. And she was the one who made the threats.''

He refused to believe that. ''No.''

''Yes. She threatened all sorts of wild things—to kill Adele, to kill Riley. To tell the world that she was carrying Caleb's child and what a rotten bastard he was. But then, in the end, she agreed to Caleb's terms. She took the check.'' He was shaking his head, but Katie just went on talking. ''She took the check when she was eight months along. But instead of sticking around to give you to Caleb when you were born, she ran off. She cashed that check. And she raised you on her own—just as you told me she did, always moving from one place to another, keeping ahead of any chance that Caleb might find her—and you.''

"No.''

She threw the envelope on the table between them. ''It's all in there. Her threatening letters, what Caleb offered, what she refused—and then eventually accepted. There's even the cancelled check for a half million dollars, complete with her endorsement on the back.''

"No. I don't believe you.'' He glared down at her.

And her face softened, suddenly, with something that might have been pity. ''It's all there. Look it over. Come to grips with the truth.'' She stood. ''We can all use a little more truth around here, and that's a plain fact. And the truth is, your mother took Caleb's money and she ran off. Where do you think she got the start-up funds for those businesses you mentioned to me once—you know, the ones that failed?''

"No,'' he said. Again. He couldn't say it enough. ''No, no…''

Katie refused to back down. ''I'm sorry, Justin. I truly am. Sorry for you, for what you've become. I think, if there's ever going to be any hope for you, you're going to have face what your mother did. And accept it. You're going to have to admit how angry you are at her. Because I know, just from the few things you said to me about her, that she made your childhood a living hell.''

*It wasn't her fault,* he thought, as he'd been thinking for his whole life. *She did the best she could....*

Too bad his old excuses for the woman who'd raised him rang so hollow now.

And Katie wasn't finished. "What Caleb did was wrong. All wrong. Using your mother, and then trying to buy her off, to cut her out of your life, to take you away from her. He was so wrong. And now he's paying for it. But don't imagine he didn't want you. Don't even try to tell yourself he walked away from *you.* He would have claimed you, would have possibly lost Adele for your sake, would have taken the chance of putting Riley's childhood in jeopardy, if your mother had kept her end of their bargain."

Justin couldn't stay upright. He sank to a chair, muttered, one last time, "No. It can't be...."

"Justin. It *is.*"

He stared up at her—at the matchless woman he'd lost to his own blindness and pride. Right then, as he began to fully understand the depths to which he'd sunk, his mother's words came to him.

*When I'm gone, you'll get your chance to make it all right.*

He saw it all then, in a blinding burst of terrible clarity that had his stomach churning, and acid rising to his throat: the truth Katie spoke of.

He'd made nothing right. He'd only made a bad situation worse.

Yes. Katie was right. His anger with his mother went deeper than he'd ever realized.

But that anger was nothing against how much he was finding he despised himself.

"Go," he said. "Please. Go now."

Katie looked uncertain. A miracle, that woman. *His* miracle, lost forever to him now. He saw in her sweet face that, in spite of everything, she was afraid. For him.

He sat up straighter. "I'm not going to do anything…drastic. I'm going to sit here and read over the stuff in this envelope. I'm going to think about what you've said to me. I need to do that alone."

She swallowed. "All right, then. You may not believe this. But I do wish you well. And I hope that, somehow, you'll find a way to make peace. With Caleb. And with your mother's memory."

He forced a twisted smile. "Goodbye, Katie."

A shudder went through her. But she lifted her head high. "Yes. All right. Goodbye."

## *Chapter Fifteen*

The next day, Justin Caldwell did something he'd never before done in his adult life. He called his office and said he had personal business to see to and he wouldn't be in.

Strange, now he thought of it. He really didn't have a personal life to speak of. He could think of only one other time when he might have needed a personal day and that was when his mother died.

But as it turned out, Ramona had died on a Saturday afternoon, so Justin had his "personal" days on the weekend and showed up at the office at nine Monday morning.

This time, the personal business in question consisted mostly of wandering around in his bathrobe, reading and rereading the letters in the envelope Katie had left with him—reading the letters and staring at the photographs of his father and mother, together.

And occasionally, picking up that cancelled check with his mother's signature on the back of it and wondering...

At his blind, thoughtless and pigheaded father.

At the selfish vengefulness of his mother.

Really, when it came down to it, blood did tell. Hadn't their son turned out to be all those things?

Blind, thoughtless, pigheaded, selfish—and vengeful.

Justin Caldwell. Biggest SOB on the planet, bar none.

The question now was: what the hell could he do about that?

All day long, wandering around his gorgeous, empty house in his bathrobe, he pondered that question. All day long, and into the evening.

It was a little after seven and he was starting to think that maybe he should make himself go into the kitchen and microwave something to put in his stomach, when the doorbell rang.

*Katie...*

His pulse started racing and his heart did something acrobatic inside his chest.

But the thrill quickly faded. It wouldn't be her. It *couldn't* be her. It was over between them. He knew it. At least in his mind. Over time, he hoped the rest of him—body, heart, soul—would learn to accept it.

Shaking his head at his own foolish yearning, he got up and went to the door.

"Mr. Caldwell. How are you?" Josiah Green stuck out a hand.

Baffled, Justin took it. They shook. "Er. What can I do for you?"

Green took in Justin's unshaved face and the bathrobe he'd never gotten around to changing out of. "Oh, my. I see I've come at an inopportune time."

It was the perfect excuse—but for some weird reason, Justin didn't take it. "Come on in."

After a moment's hesitation, Green came through the door and Justin shut it behind him. The tall, somber fellow wore a long black coat over what appeared to be the same ministerial black getup he'd worn the day Justin and Katie exchanged their fake vows. "Well. Can I take your coat?"

"Thank you." He had an envelope in his hand— an envelope like the one Katie had brought the night before. Bizarre. "Hold this, please."

Justin took the envelope and Green removed his coat and laid it over one of the two entrance hall chairs. When Justin tried to hand the envelope back, Green put up a lean, long-fingered hand. "No. That's yours."

"I don't understand."

"Ahem. Well. We shall get to it." Weirder by the minute. Green said, "Right now, I'd so enjoy a cup of nice, hot coffee."

Justin blinked. "Coffee."

"Yes. Please." Green gave him a tight little smile.

"Uh. Well, okay. This way."

They proceeded to the kitchen, where Justin set the envelope on the table and Green took a seat.

"I'll just get the coffee going."

"Bless you."

While the coffee dripped, they spoke of the weather—the warming trend had ended; snow was predicted for tomorrow—and of how Green admired Justin's lovely home.

"And, may I ask," the older man inquired with some delicacy, "where is your charming bride?"

*Katie.*

Didn't he have it bad enough, trying not to think of her, without some crazy old guy showing up at his door and asking where she was? He peered more closely at the old guy in question. "I have one question."

"Certainly. Ask away."

"What's going on here?"

Green did a little throat-clearing. "Well. Sadly, I must inform you that, while you and your bride are married in the eyes of Our Lord, the state of Montana has its own rules."

"Rules?" Justin repeated, for lack of anything better to say. He sincerely was not following.

Green tapped the envelope. "I've brought you your marriage license. I'm afraid I was somewhat remiss when I stepped forward to lead you through your vows a week ago last Saturday."

"Uh. Remiss?"

Green chided, "It appears the two of you never applied for this license. When I attempted to file it, I was told they had no record of your application. Nowadays, I regret to inform you, the blessing of a man of God is simply not enough."

Without a doubt. Weirder by the minute. "You mean you actually are…a minister?"

Green snapped his thin shoulders back. "Well, of course I'm a minister."

Justin put up a hand. "Look. Sorry."

"Ahem. Well. All right, then. Your apology is graciously accepted."

"Thanks. But I thought you understood. That 'wedding' was a reenactment. It wasn't—"

"There are no reenactments in the eyes of heaven," Green cut in reprovingly before Justin could finish. "One does. Or one doesn't. You did. So don't mistake me, young man, Katherine *is* your wife in the eyes of the Lord, and those eyes, as you should very well know, are the ones that truly matter. Ahem." He frowned. "Now, where was I?"

As if Justin had a clue. "Something about applying for a license, I think.…"

"Yes. Well, and that is the crux of it. You and Katherine must go immediately to the county clerk's office and apply for a valid license, then the marriage can be resolemnified and all will be well. I will be pleased to perform the ceremony for you, if you would like me to do so. But any ordained minister will certainly suffice. Legally, you can simply say your vows at the courthouse, if that's your bent." Green put a dark emphasis on the word, *bent,* making it crystal clear that he felt all marriages should be *solemnified* by a man of God.

And Justin hadn't the faintest idea what to say to all this. It seemed to him that the old guy might be a little off in the head—in a harmless sort of way. So he simply announced, "Coffee's ready."

"Wonderful. Two sugars. No cream."

Fifteen minutes later, after handing Justin a card, "In case you should wish to request my services for the ceremony," Green put on his big, black coat and went out the door.

He left the envelope on the kitchen table.

Justin tried to ignore it. But it was like his mother's letters, like the photographs of her and Caleb, like that damn cancelled check.

The envelope on the kitchen table would not be ignored.

He microwaved some canned spaghetti and sat at the table to eat it, his gaze tracking to the waiting envelope after every bite.

Finally, muttering a string of very bad words, he pushed his plate away and grabbed the damn thing.

He pulled out the license and stared down at it. "Katie…" he whispered to the empty room. With a shaking finger, he traced the letters in her name. "I love you."

He said the three impossible words and he knew they were true.

Out of all the lies, all the dirty tricks, out of everything he'd done so very wrong.

This one truth remained.

He loved Katie Fenton.

He loved her.

It was all wrong and it was too late.

But that didn't change the basic truth.

He loved Katie.

And now it was up to him do what he could—though it would never be enough—to make the wrongs he'd done right.

## Chapter Sixteen

At eight-thirty on Monday morning, Justin entered the Thunder Canyon Ski Resort Project offices through the front door.

He found Caleb's secretary standing behind her desk in the reception area, packing a large cardboard box. She glanced up and gasped.

He tried a friendly smile. "Alice, isn't it?"

Alice didn't smile back. Instead, in a clear attempt to show the evil man before her exactly how she felt about the current situation, she adjusted her thick-lensed glasses more firmly on the bridge of her pointed nose and dropped a bronze paperweight into the box—hard. "We have until nine," she announced loftily. "Certainly you can wait until then."

He spoke gently. "Alice. You were never asked to leave."

"I prefer *Ms.* Pockstead—and I'm Mr. Douglas's assistant. He goes, I go."

Justin nodded. "Ms. Pockstead, I completely understand." He waited while she threw a stapler and a red coffee mug with dancing white hearts on it into the box. Then he cautiously cleared his throat. She sent him a hot glare. "What *is* it?"

"I wonder, is Caleb in?"

For that, he got another gasp of outrage and a tightly muttered, "The unmitigated nerve of some people…" She tossed some pencils and a ruler in the box, simmering where she stood.

Justin moved a step closer and injected a note of command into his next question. "I asked you, is he in?"

Ms. Pockstead picked up a letter opener and stabbed the air in the direction of the hallway that led to Caleb's private office. "See for yourself."

"Thank you."

She muttered something. It wasn't, *You're welcome.*

The door to Caleb's office stood slightly ajar. Justin hesitated in front of it. There was silence from inside the room beyond.

But he couldn't stand there forever. With some reluctance, he lifted a hand and tapped lightly.

"What the hell now?" grumbled the gruff voice from the other side. "It's open."

Justin flattened his palm against the door and pushed it inward.

Caleb sat at his desk surrounded by open, half-packed boxes. He appeared, at the moment, to be doing nothing about filling them.

He glanced up. Something sparked in his eyes—and then went cold. "Justin."

"Hello, Caleb."

They regarded each other. Justin had no idea what, exactly, he should say. He got the impression Caleb was having the same problem.

Finally, Caleb put out a hand at the guest chairs facing the desk. "Sit. If you've a mind to."

It seemed like as good a suggestion as any. Justin strode over, moved a box to the floor, and took one of the chairs.

They looked at each other some more. Eventually, Caleb inclined his head at the boxes surrounding him. "Sitting down on the job, I'm afraid. But I'm working on it."

How to begin, Justin was thinking.

Hell. *Where* to begin...

Caleb must have been pondering the same questions, because, again, he spoke first. "Katie said she told you...everything."

Justin found the best he could manage right then was a nod.

Caleb nodded, too. A lot of nodding going on. Oh, yeah. They were a couple of nodding fools.

Caleb said, "Well, then. It's all out in the open." He grunted. "I have to keep reminding myself how that's good. I..." He paused, seeming to seek the right words. Evidently he found them, or close enough. He said, "I understand now, why you did what you did at the meeting last week. Given the

circumstances, I've got no damn problem with it.''
He raised both hands, indicating the office—the
whole ski resort project. ''In a half an hour or so, it's
all yours.'' Justin started to speak, but Caleb cut him
off before he got a word out. ''What you did to Katie,
though. No damn excuse for that.''

''I know,'' Justin said.

Caleb stared at him, narrowed-eyed. And then he
grunted again. ''Hope you do. You threw away a
good one. The very best, as a matter of fact.''

''You don't have to tell me.''

''Hell. I guess I don't. I can see it in your eyes.''
He sat back. ''You love my girl, don't you?''

Justin reminded himself that he was through with
lies. He gave Caleb the painful truth. ''Yes. I do. I
love her.''

Caleb pondered that for a moment, then he
shrugged. ''Well. Evidently you're not as big of a fool
as I'd been thinking—and don't go imagining you're
the only one who's trifled with a good and loving
heart. I've done the same thing, as you damn well
know.''

Justin said nothing. He was realizing that here was
another way he was like this man who'd fathered him.

''Your mother,'' Caleb said softly. ''She was a
good woman. A good woman done wrong. She
couldn't…get past that, what I did to her, that's all.''

Justin waved a hand. ''She's gone now.''

''Don't judge her.''

''I'm working on it. Your…wife?''

It took Caleb a moment to answer that one. ''Addy
and me, we've been together too long to give up now.

She's not happy with me. But I've got hopes that someday…'' He let that sentence finish itself. ''Riley, though. I don't know. He's not in a mood for forgiving.''

''Give him time.''

''Time.'' Caleb chuckled, a dry sound with no real laughter in it. ''Well.'' He stood. ''Better get this junk packed up.''

Justin stood, too. ''Put it back where it came from.'' Caleb blinked. And Justin continued, ''I put my man on something else. This is your project and you're fully capable of seeing it through to a successful conclusion. I'm leaving it to you, where it always belonged. And I'll be pulling out completely, as soon as I find some other solid investors to step in and fill the gap.''

Caleb sank to his chair again. ''You don't have to do this.''

''Yeah. Yeah, I do—and don't even think of trying to turn me down. I'm out. And you're going to be needed here.''

Caleb looked up at him. ''Don't pull out. Stay in.''

Justin frowned. ''That's probably a bad idea.''

''No. It's a good one. An excellent one. Stay in. We'll make a little money together. We'll give a shot in the arm to the local economy and we'll…start getting to know each other.''

''You want that?''

''Yeah, I do. I want that a lot.''

''Let me think about it.''

''Take as long as you need. Just be sure the answer's yes.''

* * *

Caleb called him at home at seven that night. Skipping right over anything resembling hello, he said, "So. You made up your mind yet?"

Justin couldn't hold back a chuckle. "I thought I was supposed to take all the time I needed."

"You've had time enough. Say yes."

He'd already decided, anyway. "All right. I'm in."

"Good. You have a nice night, now." And the line went dead.

Justin took the phone away from his ear and stared at it, shaking his head. Then, gently, he set it down.

He turned for the table where the remains of his solitary dinner waited to be cleared off. The job only took a few minutes.

Then he went out to his study, where he booted up his laptop and settled in for a few hours of work on a new project he was putting together.

The doorbell rang at five to eight. He hit the save key and got up to answer.

The last person in the world he'd ever expected to see was waiting beyond the front door.

"Katie." Damned if his heart didn't do a forward roll.

She looked up at him, brown eyes gleaming, soft cheeks flushed. There was snow on her shoulders, sparkling in her chestnut hair. She brushed at it. "Caleb said you wanted to see me."

His mind was a fog of hope and yearning. "Caleb…"

Her sweet face fell. "He…was wrong?"

"No," he said—so forcefully that she jumped back.

He tried again, more gently. "No. Caleb was absolutely right."

"Well. So, then?" She managed a hopeful smile. "Do you think maybe I might come in?"

He gaped at her, and then, at last, he remembered to speak. "Yeah. Absolutely. Come in."

## Chapter Seventeen

He took her coat, his heart racing like a runaway train at the mere fact that she'd handed it over.

Because, after all, if she let him take her coat, that meant she would stay, didn't it? At least for a little while.

He shook the remaining snow off it, set it on the entry hall chair and led her through to the great room. "Sit down. Please."

She perched on a long sofa. "I…" She seemed to be doing a lot of swallowing. He understood. His throat kept locking up, too. She tried again. "Emelda tells me you made a generous donation to the Historical Society—very generous, is what she said."

He looked down at her, astounded. Amazed. Was there ever a woman so damned, incredibly beautiful?

No. He was sure of it. She was one of a kind.

"Justin?"

"Yeah?"

"You're staring."

He gulped again. "Uh. Sorry. Listen, want some coffee? I made it an hour ago, but it should still be okay."

Her gaze scanned his face, sweetly. Hungrily.

Or was that just him seeing what he wanted to see?

"Coffee," she repeated.

"Yeah. You think?"

"Yes. Okay. I'll have some."

"Stay right there."

She let out a nervous little giggle. "Well, Justin. Where would I go?"

He raced for the kitchen, poured the damn coffee— two mugfuls, since it seemed a little rude to let her drink hers alone. He remembered she liked cream and splashed some into hers. Then he rushed back to the great room, coffee sloshing across the Kelim area rugs as he went.

When he got back to her, she was standing at a narrow section of wall between two wide windows, looking at...

Damn. She was never supposed to see that.

He'd never dared to imagine she'd set foot in his house again, or he wouldn't have put the thing up.

She turned to him. "Justin? That's the fake license. From that day at the town hall."

"Uh…" He scooted over and plunked the mugs down on a low table. Coffee, still sloshing, dribbled down the sides.

"It is, isn't it?"

He rubbed his hands together, brushing off the coffee he'd spilled on them. "Well, yeah. That's what it is."

She came toward him. He watched her as she moved, devouring her with his eyes. When she stood about a foot from him, she asked, "Where did you get it?"

Her scent swam around him. His fingers itched to grab for her. To keep them busy, he gestured at the table. "Coffee. There you go."

"Justin." Her voice was so soft. And the tiniest, most radiant smile had begun at the corners of that mouth he wanted so badly to kiss. She touched his arm. He felt that touch all the way down to the center of his soul. "Where did you get it?"

"Josiah Green."

"Our fake minister?"

"Turns out he wasn't a fake. A little eccentric maybe, but not a fake."

"You're kidding. The real thing?"

He managed a nod.

"He gave you the license?"

"He did."

"But why?"

His throat loosened a little and he told her about Green's visit, about the things the old guy had said.

She hadn't removed her hand from his arm. Her touch burned him. He was going up in flames.

She said, "Caleb says you love me. Is that true?"

Struck mute again, he could only nod.

"Oh, Justin…"

He knew she needed more than that. Hell, *he* needed more than that. "I... Katie, I know the things I did were wrong. Unforgivable, even. I know I blew it. Lost you. Lost the best thing that ever happened to me. That's why I had that fake license framed. I hung it on the wall, where I'd see it all the time. Where I'd remember, what might have been. If only I hadn't—"

"Justin."

"What, damn it?"

"Close your eyes."

"I don't—"

"Just do it. Close your eyes."

"Hell." But he did what she asked.

And as he stood there, blind before her, he felt her warm breath against his neck, felt the living, sweet-scented heat of her.

She whispered, "Personally, I *believe*. In forgiveness. I believe in hope. And faith. And..."

"Wishes," he whispered. He didn't know where that word came from. Or maybe he did.

"Yes." It came out on a gentle breath. "Yes." That *yes* shivered through him. He felt it echo, in the beating of his heart. "Wishes," she said. "Wishes that can come true. If you..."

"Make them."

"If you're—"

"Done with lying. With dirty tricks."

"Oh, yes. That's right. Wishes and hope and faith. And forgiveness. I do believe in them, Justin. I believe in *you*."

It was too much.

It was everything.

Every wish he never dared to make.

Every dream he'd never known how to believe in.

All of it. Right here.

Everything. Katie.

She put her hands on his shoulders. A shudder went through him. And he felt her lift up, on tiptoe, to place a kiss on each of his lowered eyelids, one and then the other.

And that did it. He couldn't keep still one second longer.

He opened his eyes and he reached for her.

With a happy, willing cry, she came into his arms.

He lifted her high against his chest and, holding her close, knowing he'd never, ever let her go, he carried her out of the high-ceilinged room, away from all those dark windows, down a long hallway to his bedroom.

They undressed each other, quickly, hands shaking, sharing kisses and nervous, eager glances—soft whispers, and yet more kisses.

At last she stood before him, slim and proud, her body gleaming, pale and pearly, in the dimness.

"Katie..."

She held her head high, and she looked right back at him. "Justin."

He swept her up again, carried her to the bed and laid her down on it.

And he kissed her. Kissed every fragrant, smooth,

beautiful inch of her, lingering at her breasts, her belly, her thighs.

He kissed his way up them, and then he parted her and he kissed her some more, there, at the wet, hot feminine heart of her, as she called out his name, her soft fingers tangled in his hair.

When she came, he drank her, taking her release inside of him. So sweet. So exactly what he'd never dared, till now, to dream of.

She touched his shoulders, reaching, urging him up over her. He settled—so carefully, his body aching for her—between her open thighs.

He looked down at her, met those shining eyes. "Your first time?"

She pressed her lips together and nodded. "It's what I want, though. You. You're what I want."

He didn't want to leave her. Not even for a moment. But there was protection to consider. "I should..." Her sweet heat was all around him, her body pliant, ready. "We need to..."

She caught his face between her hands. "What Reverend Green said...we're married. Right? How did you say he said it?"

He groaned. "In the eyes of heaven."

"Oh, yes. I...well, don't say I'm crazy. But I like that. I *believe* in that. And if there was a baby..."

A baby. Incredible.

She asked, so softly, "Would that be all right with you?"

It *was* crazy. Absolutely insane. But he found that it would. He swallowed. Hard. And he managed to croak out, "Yeah."

And she wrapped her satiny legs around him. "Then it's okay...it's all right."

He made himself go slowly, pushing in just a little, holding still...waiting.

It was the sweetest kind of agony—the pleasure, within the pain. He held still and he kissed her—eyes, cheeks, nose, chin. He whispered, "Slowly...slowly..."

She moaned and held him, her sleek body moving, then going still. He pushed in farther—felt resistance and then, at last, the slow, gentle opening.

Welcoming.

It took forever. An eternity of slow, controlled degrees.

Until at last, he felt himself fully within her. "Don't...move..." he pleaded on a ragged sigh.

But she had other ideas. "I...I have to. Oh, Justin. I need..." And her hips began to rock him. "I need...you. You. Only."

He kissed the words from her lips and gave them back to her. "Only you."

The pleasure took over, all the words flew away. They rode an endless, swirling river of it, of pleasure. It sucked him into a whirlpool. He went spinning...

Spinning.

And then it centered down.

Down into Katie. Into the soft pulsing of her heat and wetness all around him.

He let out a cry, tossing his head back. And she cried out in answer.

The rest was soft sighs, tender caresses.

"I love you," she whispered.

And he could only smile.

\*   \*   \*

It was an hour later when he dared to suggest, "Marry me. Again."

She looked up at him from under the sable fringe of her lashes. "Yes. I will."

"Soon," he demanded.

"Oh, absolutely. And in the town hall. With everyone in Thunder Canyon invited. And the Reverend Green presiding. What do you think?"

"I think, yes. Beyond a shadow of a doubt. No conditions. Yes."

"Just one thing."

"Anything. Everything."

She laughed then, and the sound banished all darkness. It filled up the world with golden light.

"Promise me," she said. "No free beer."

So he promised, sealing it—and all the other, more important promises—with a tender kiss.

## *Epilogue*

On the first Saturday in February, Katie and Justin said their vows for the second time, in the town hall. In spite of the blizzard gathering force outside, the old hall was packed. The bride, radiant in white satin, had asked Caleb to give her away. Riley stood up as Justin's best man. The eccentric Reverend Green, looking pleased with himself *and* the proceedings, officiated.

When the reverend asked Katie if she would take Justin to be her lawfully wedded husband—to love him, to honor and to cherish him for as long as they both should live—Katie, so often soft-spoken, especially in crowds, answered loud and clear.

"I will." Her brown eyes shone. Her face was suffused with a glow of pure joy.

After the vow-sealing kiss, the party began, right

there in the hall. Montana Gold, a band of local boys, took the stage and a generous buffet, laid out on long tables, eased the appetites of the assembled guests. Beer was limited, as per the bride's instructions.

But there was champagne, and it flowed freely. When the band took its first break, the toasting began. Caleb was delivering a long speech about true love and happiness and getting through the tough times, when Cameron Stevenson's seven-year-old, Erik, sneaked up on the stage and started banging on the keyboards. Caleb sent a quelling look over his shoulder at the boy, who quickly moved on to the drums. With a crashing sound, the high hat tumbled to the stage.

Cam went after Erik, then, and led him off, but everyone laughed and burst into raucous clapping and catcalls.

After the toasts and speeches, Katie and Justin cut the enormous cake. As Adele supervised the cake distribution, the band took over again for a second set.

Several men pitched in to push the tables back against the wall and Caleb led Katie out on the floor. They danced, but not for long. Justin cut in.

As the citizens of Thunder Canyon applauded the bride and groom's first dance, Justin whispered, "Happy?"

Katie looked up at him, all her love shining in her eyes. "Happy doesn't even begin to describe it."

He pulled her closer. She settled her head against his shoulder. Other couples joined them, filling the floor.

When that dance ended, the band swung into another number. Katie stayed where she wanted to be: held close in Justin's loving arms. The band played on. They danced every dance.

It was no time at all until Montana Gold announced their second break. Justin took Katie's hand and led her to the sidelines, where a special table had been set up specifically for the bride and groom and family.

Adele was just serving them each a piece of cake, when Cam Stevenson edged his way toward them through the milling crowd.

One look at Cam's too-pale face, and Katie knew there was trouble.

Cam bent down to ask her, "Have you seen Erik?"

She shook her head. "But he's probably out in the foyer. I saw a bunch of the kids heading that way."

"No. He's not there. I looked."

"Did you look—?"

"Everywhere, damn it. I've been all through the building."

Justin was already on his feet. "Come on. Let's look again. He can't have gone far...."

\* \* \* \* \*

*Don't miss the second book in the exciting* MONTANA *continuity.* All He Ever Wanted *by Allison Leigh is out in June 2006.*

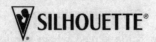

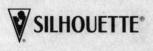

**▼ SILHOUETTE®**

0506/23b

# SPECIAL EDITION™

## ALL HE EVER WANTED
### by Allison Leigh

*Montana*

When young Erik fell down a mine shaft, he was saved
by brave and beautiful Faith Taylor. Faith was amazed
by the feelings Erik's handsome father, Cameron, awoke.
But was Cam ready to find a new happiness?

## PLAYING WITH FIRE by Arlene James

*Lucky in Love*

Struggling hairstylist Valerie Blunt had a lot on her mind
—well, mainly the infuriatingly attractive Fire Marshal
Ian Keene. Ian set Valerie alight whenever he was near…

## BECAUSE A HUSBAND
## IS FOREVER
### by Marie Ferrarella

*The Cameo*

Talk show host Dakota Delaney agreed to allow
bodyguard Ian Russell to shadow her. But she hadn't
counted on the constant battling or that he would want to
take hold of her safety—and her heart.

**Don't miss out!**
**On sale from 19th May 2006**

*Available at WHSmith, Tesco, ASDA, Borders, Eason,
Sainsbury's and most bookshops*

*www.silhouette.co.uk*

# FREE

## 4 BOOKS AND A SURPRISE GIFT!

We would like to take this opportunity to thank you for reading this Silhouette® book by offering you the chance to take FOUR more specially selected titles from the Special Edition™ series absolutely FREE! We're also making this offer to introduce you to the benefits of the Reader Service™—

- ★ **FREE home delivery**
- ★ **FREE gifts and competitions**
- ★ **FREE monthly Newsletter**
- ★ **Books available before they're in the shops**
- ★ **Exclusive Reader Service offers**

Accepting these FREE books and gift places you under no obligation to buy; you may cancel at any time, even after receiving your free shipment. Simply complete your details below and return the entire page to the address below. You don't even need a stamp!

**YES!** Please send me 4 free Special Edition books and a surprise gift. I understand that unless you hear from me, I will receive 6 superb new titles every month for just £3.10 each, postage and packing free. I am under no obligation to purchase any books and may cancel my subscription at any time. The free books and gift will be mine to keep in any case.

E6ZEE

Ms/Mrs/Miss/Mr..........................................Initials ...............................
BLOCK CAPITALS PLEASE

Surname ...........................................................................................

Address ...........................................................................................

.............................................................................................................

.............................................................Postcode ...............................

Send this whole page to:
The Reader Service, FREEPOST CN81, Croydon, CR9 3WZ